ZOË TROPE

ZOË TROPE

Amanda Prantera

BLOOMSBURY

First published in Great Britain 1996

This paperback edition published 1997

Copyright © 1996 by Amanda Prantera

The moral right of the author
has been asserted

Bloomsbury Publishing Plc, 38 Soho Square,
London W1V 5DF

A CIP catalogue record for this book
is available from the British Library

ISBN 0 7475 3164 1

Typeset by Hewer Text Composition Services, Edinburgh
Printed in Great Britain by Clays Ltd, St Ives plc

FOR JILL

INTRODUCTION

I was ten when my grandmother died – the prominent one, the one who played such an important part in my early upbringing – and although I was very fond of her and knew I was very fond of her, the strongest emotion I remember feeling was relief, almost joyous in its intensity.

It sat on me awkwardly, this feeling, during the hushed, delicate days that followed the funeral. I could see that nobody else shared it and did everything I could to hide it from them in consequence, but nevertheless it was there, stashed away somewhere inside me, waiting to break out and trick me into smiles and skips in front of the red-eyed maids and long-faced visitors and under the faraway gaze of my grieving, hypocrite father. I had to be very careful about the way I moved, the way I spoke, even the way I set about my food.

The feeling puzzled me a little too, perhaps even shamed me (because after years of training from my grandmother herself, conventional patterns of behaviour were becoming more familiar to me and I knew this was no way to react to the death of a close relative: with a light heart and an almost uncontrollable desire to dance), but I was unable to discover its cause until the third day after the funeral, when, solicitors departed and visits of condolence dwindling, my father and I sat down to our first solitary meal together in my grandmother's house, or what had formerly been my grandmother's house but now seemed to belong to no one. Then, suddenly, everything fell into place.

Of course, I thought to myself, relishing the silence that lay between us and unable this time to do anything about hiding my smile, it is over, that is what it is, the midday wrangling, the torture, the agony is over. I am sorry for Grandmother and I will miss her badly in many other less critical moments of the day, but now that she is no longer with us it means that we will be able to eat our lunches in peace.

I said nothing to my father, but he smiled back at me – his first smile in days – and I reckoned he must know what I was thinking. Strangely I didn't blame him, neither for his past cruelty (because it was always he who started it, I knew this from my grandmother who would cradle me in her arms afterwards and repeat this into my hair until it became quite wet from her tears), nor for his present duplicity in pretending to be sad (wasn't I guilty of the same thing myself?). I was just relieved, beyond words, beyond blame, beyond sadness, beyond everything, that it was over.

'When will you realize you are breaking my heart with this life you lead?'

'Your heart? You haven't got a heart, you've got an octopus lodged in your chest, that's what you've got. Suck, suck, cling, cling, bind, bind.'

'Why do you talk if it is only to wound me?'

'I talk because there's nothing else to do in this mausoleum of a house.'

'Ah! But this mausoleum is a convenient place to park your child, isn't it? *Isn't* it? While you and your wife go gadding around to parties and race meetings and goodness knows what, behaving like children yourselves. When will you grow up, the pair of you, I would like to know? When will you learn to shoulder your own burdens?'

'I never knew you looked on Zoë as a burden, but if that's the way you feel, then the answer's simple. She will come straight back home with me today and never again set foot in this godforsaken place.' (To me, but not with sufficient conviction to move me from my chair): 'Go and pack your things, Zo, we're not wanted here, we're off.'

'Ah!' (But with a different emphasis this time, the 'a' much longer, making it sound more like a sob.) 'You would do that to me? Deprive me of the child in order to spite me? You know, I truly believe you would, however much it might interfere with your trips to Deauville and Monte Carlo. But I'm not going to allow it. My duty to Zoë comes first. I may have failed over your upbringing, but I am not going to fail over hers, oh, no, no, no.'

'Duty? You call it duty? I call it blackmail and lust for power. Incredible, under that flawless exterior, what a wicked old woman you are. No wonder your husband chose to live in a different continent. I would do the same if I could afford it.'

'If you worked you might be able to afford it. Try it and see. Try working for just one day and see what comes of it. Who knows, you might develop some self-esteem.'

'The day I free myself of you I might develop some self-esteem. Until then I can only despise myself.'

'Despise yourself? For what? For coming to see me for one miserable hour a day? For giving me the crumbs of your time? What a terrible, terrible thing to say to your own mother in your daughter's hearing! What a cruel, unforgivable thing!'

'That's right, turn on the tears. When all else fails fall back on tears! Blub, blub, blub, poor me, poor me. Poor you, be damned! You're as strong as steel, and as tough as old nails. As tough as this dreadful meat you expect me to eat. I've had enough. Of the meat, of you, of this house full of old female crows, of everything. I'm off. For real this time and don't expect me back in a hurry because I won't be coming.'

Silence broken by sniffs on the one side of the table and snorts on the other. Then:

Sniff. 'That looks like a new wristwatch you're wearing. Very nice. Very smart.'

Snort. 'Cartier. I'm glad you like it.'

'I'm glad *you* like it. If I had a daughter who had grown out of all her clothes and a mother who could hardly afford to buy hay for her bloodstock, I'm not sure I would derive much enjoyment from a new Cartier watch. But there.'

'Wait a minute, what do you mean, buy hay? I thought you grew hay. I thought that was one of the reasons you insisted on hanging on to so much land. Don't tell me now, with all these acres of useless grass, you're actually going out and buying the stuff on the market?'

'You don't understand. But how could you? You never take an interest in anything that goes on in the place. Our hay this year went musty and was unfit for horses, so Tucker had to sell it off cheaply for cattle fodder. He was very lucky to get the price he did. There was a risk at one point that we might have to burn it in order to be rid of it.'

'My dear Clara, as the judge said to the jury or the doctor to the madman or whichever it was, if you believe that you'll believe anything. Tucker has been rooking you for the past twenty years and will go on rooking you for twenty more to come. He's sold your hay at top price, given you next to nothing for it, and now he's no doubt replacing it with the cheapest, mustiest stuff he can get, which you will again pay top price for. And I don't blame him either. Some people are *born* to be swindled.'

'And some people are born to do nothing but stir up trouble. Tucker may take a little commission money from the dealers here and there, but if he does it's his affair and I don't want to know about it. If I sacked him I would have no one to turn to. No man, that is. And an old, frail woman like me needs the support of a man in this cut-throat business.'

'What am I then? A boy, is that what you wanted to say? A hopeless thirty-two-year-old boy who'll never grow up? Well, maybe I am, but if I am then who's to blame? Let's put this one to Zoë. Zo, if I put bricks on your head to stop you growing, and gave you nothing but baby-food so you couldn't cut your teeth, and dressed you in nappies, and kept you in a cradle, whose fault would it be if you never grew up, eh? Yours or mine? Eh?'

'You don't even dress her in nappies. *I* dress her. *I* dress her with *my* money while you treat yourself to watches from Cartier.'

'A taste I must have inherited from my father. Did you go on at him in the same way, I wonder? Or did you merely open up your great blue eyes and look reproachful? Poor Eddie, how I feel for him! No wonder he ran. No wonder he didn't come back, not even to die.'

'What do you mean? What has Edward got to do with it? Let me have a look. That's not his watch by any chance, is it?'

'Yes, Clara. Eddie's watch, bought at great expense at

Cartier's together with your diamond earrings, in the days when hay was not exactly at the top of your shopping list. Don't say you didn't recognize it?'

'What a mean trick to play! You know my eyes are failing along with everything else.'

'Serves you right. A mean trick for a mean old woman.'

'A careful old woman. Where would you be if it wasn't for me? In the hands of the money-lenders, that's where. *Back* in the hands of the money-lenders. Or do I have to remind you, here in front of your own daughter, about that business . . .?'

'You don't have to remind me of anything, much as you'd like to, because I'm leaving. Right now, and this time it's for good. I'm leaving you like everyone has always left you, and it's no good crying because it just doesn't work any more. You've overplayed your hand as far as the tears are concerned, you can bloody well drown in them for all I care.'

All this was over. I no longer had to sit silent between them, feeling myself tugged first one way and then the other, listening to the crescendo of their terrible, whiplash words, waiting for the inevitable moment when my father would make his daily exit and I would be used as blotting paper for my grandmother's tears.

My relief at a problem solved, a complication eliminated from my life, was enormous. We had a very nice quiet lunch that day, or so it seemed to me, my father and I. He didn't eat much, but then, as he had repeatedly pointed out to Grandmother, he never had liked the food that was served up at her table.

When we had finished and the coffee was brought in

(I don't think he'd ever reached the coffee stage before, not the drinking of it anyway), he took me on his knee and told me that maybe we were going to come and live in this house now, and asked me if I liked the idea, and if so what changes I would like to see made to my bedroom, and things like that. Comfortable, ordinary, everyday things, untinged by the note of melodrama I had come to associate with him at lunchtimes. Afterwards my hair felt wet and I thought for a moment he had been using it for the same purpose as Grandmother did, but decided he must simply have spilt some of his coffee on the top of my head.

Only a few days later, however, my certainties about this and indeed many other things were taken away from me by the chance words of an emotionally inclined female visitor, who, on her way out after seeing my father, drew me deep into the pile of her fur coat and whispered, 'Stay close to him, Zoë. He needs all the help you can give him. He and Clara loved one another so much, you see. So much, so much. I have never known a mother and son so passionately fond of one another.'

It was on the tip of my tongue to correct her and inform her of the real state of affairs that had existed between my grandmother and father, but something, some instinct, some flash of recognition, intervened to keep me silent and nod pseudo-wisely instead. After she had gone I remember standing for several moments in the cloud of the woman's perfume and feeling my thoughts, my loyalties, so mobile over the past days, settle into yet another pattern. So it was *love*, I said to myself many times over, until I was sure I believed it. That was love. That is love. That is how people who love each other behave. Who would ever have thought it?

It is not my habit to blame others for my own muddles, but in partial explanation of what follows, it does sometimes strike me that this was perhaps not the clearest of introductions to the subject.

JEREMY

Jeremy's reputation reached me long before he did, and on the basis of it I already loved him. Humbly, respectfully, long-distance, the way you were supposed to love Jesus.

Like Jesus's too his image had a kind of halo around it in my mind, a golden light caused, I think, originally by my hearing of a brilliant-threaded waistcoat he was entitled to wear in his last year at school for special merits, but subsequently by more standard allusions on the part of adults to golden boys and golden futures and *jeunesse dorée* and all the rest.

He was, going by hearsay anyway, one of those rare people who reap round-the-spectrum admiration and nothing but. Girls gazed but didn't dare think of him as prey: he flew too high. His male friends loved him on account of this, and because for them he travelled just a stratum lower, brushing them with his wings and catching them up in his flight. Older people's faces grew nostalgic and strangely respectful when they spoke of him, as if he reminded them of forgotten heroes, forgotten virtues (although his title may have had something to do with it too). Young people's lit up with a different kind of respect: for all his old world appeal, Jeremy was cool, hip, with-it, or whatever the current shibboleth of approval was at the time.

When at last I met him it was at a dance in the country, and he was sitting in an armchair in the corner of the room, a glass of champagne in his hand. The evening dress of the period for men constrained and penguinized its wearers; it was difficult to look as if you had chosen to wear it, still more difficult to look as if you were happy with your choice. But on Jeremy the formal garb sat rightly, almost racily. He had style. And all the charm and sweetness of his advertisement.

We got on uncannily well from the first moment. We talked and it was like old friends talking. We danced and it was as if we had never done anything else. We spun round the floor in each other's arms till we were sated with this kind of rhythmic silent togetherness, and then we spun round the room hand in hand laughing and chattering, picking up more champagne glasses and downing them, raiding the buffet for strawberries, grazing briefly a group of friends we had in common, and then on, to another. Showing ourselves off.

I had a feeling of certainty and pride. I knew little of sentimental attachments between the sexes – how they started, how they progressed, how they were conducted on the physical plane – but despite my ignorance it was as if I had always expected my own pairing-off, when it happened, to be like this: optimal, effortless, stainless. A coming together of unicorns, or some other graceful type of beast unhampered by existential ballast.

When our whirlings led us out on to a darkened terrace where a definitely steamier and less prettified atmosphere seemed to reign than in the ballroom, and when Jeremy pulled me urgently down on to a *chaise-longue* on top of him and began exploring my mouth with his champagne-tasting tongue, I was not dismayed. Anything but. Here, among sighs and whispers and glowing cigarette ends, was where we belonged. With the lovers, with the adults. And whatever place my own predestined partner chose, and whatever he chose to do in it, was surely right.

His mouth was *very* alcohol-tasting, though, and his face and hands were very hot. He had had a lot to drink. Could it be he was having difficulty holding his liquor? Impossible: to a hero of Jeremy's calibre that sort of thing didn't happen. He was just impassioned, like I was myself; drunk with the joy of our meeting.

His scalding hands pushed me away from him a little and fumbled with the bodice of my dress, tugging at it frontways until the whalebones which supported it doubled back on themselves suddenly, freeing my breasts and leaving me practically naked to the waist. I was about to right this regrettable state of affairs, thinking it due to a mistake on his part and cursing the mechanics of the strapless ballgown (which did things like that if you weren't careful, I'd seen it happen to one poor girl during a reel), when his fingers latched on to the tips of both my breasts like crab pincers, and a streak of pleasure shot through me, so sweet and sizzling that I could have gasped.

Perhaps I did. This was no mistake, no, this too was absolutely right. Oh Christmas! How did he know how to do these things? Because he knew everything, that was why. Because he was Jeremy, the golden one, the cool, the brainy, the idol of the mums, who held the world in his hand. And who now held me, by the very core of my being from the feel of it, and in whose hands from the feel of it I belonged.

My spine arched backwards of its own accord so that

I could better deliver my breasts – not very big, not the melon size I would have liked, more the half-a-grapefruit – into his possession. It was strange, I had no learning, and yet my body seemed quite confident and reliable. As long as I followed the pleasure-streak I felt I could depend on it not to shame me by doing the wrong thing. (Like covering up my breasts when the dress flipped. That would have been awful.)

'Zoë,' he said from under me in a funny growly voice after a little while had passed. No, it wasn't 'Zoë', it was 'Zoë?' with a question mark. It seemed a funny time for questions. 'You're a whore, aren't you, Zoë?'

It seemed an even funnier time for questions like this. I knew a family called Hoare, but they were not relations. I didn't know what to say.

'Aren't you?' he repeated, pinching my breasts so hard that the sweet sensation fused with another, much bitterer, and then stopped. 'Answer me. Aren't you? You're a whore, a twat, a right little twat?'

This second name was unfamiliar to me, but I knew instinctively that it was not a family one and not a nice one. Something was going very wrong between us, had already gone very wrong between us. Jeremy had spoken so loudly that there were movements in the darkness, faint risings and shiftings as the couples on either side began to change the focus of their attention, and then a deep after-overture hush as they waited for the piece proper to commence.

They were not disappointed. Like vomit (which I think also came out of his mouth at some point, but I was being shepherded away by then by older people and fussed over and shielded, and can't really say for sure), a jet of ugly, acrid words started to pour out into the night. Plato says we recognize things because we have seen them in ideal form in some other existence. I don't know about this, nor can I imagine what 'ideal' form such words might once have had, but luckily I did recognize them. Enough, anyway, to know that they were weapons aimed against me, and to recoil from them and their speaker, and to cover myself up again, just in time before the terrace lights went on and a group of uncomfortable onlookers began to assemble round our chair.

'I say! Steady on! What's come over him? Now that's a bit much! Now, now, now, enough of that, enough of that! Someone go and fetch a soda siphon, or an ice bucket, that'll soon fix him!' While the other words, Jeremy's, continued to fly free into the air like conjuror's doves, scattering their dirt in all directions.

My acquaintance, if such you can call it, with Jeremy ended here, as swiftly as it had begun. After that last glimpse of him struggling hard as Laocoön with goodness-knows-what private snakes, I never saw him again, though I heard of him from time to time through friends: I believe he married young (which surprises me) and went into the wine trade (which doesn't). The morning after the upset I learnt, from overheard whispers of 'shame' and 'disgrace' and 'bad showing', as my host discussed the matter with his wife over the breakfast table, that the society that had so prized this glittering young member was now coming down on him heavily, and perhaps would continue to do so for some time and with some relish, but I was never tempted myself to join in the blame. To me the matter was simple: Jeremy had needed me to be innocent, and for some reason which I was indeed too innocent to know, I had disappointed him. Illogically perhaps – but then logic loses all its muscle in the presence of a paradox anyway – I resolved in the future to steer clear of public schoolboys, current or ex. That was all.

ADRIAN

So much for resolves. My next attraction was to a public schoolboy too: another glamour-tom, similar to Jeremy in almost every surface respect except that his father, instead of being a peer, was a philosopher. A real one (if there is such a thing), a professional one, a famous one.

The boy's name was Adrian. Again I met him at a dance, only this time it was not a relaxed country affair for young people to let off steam at, but a grand and rather forbidding ball in London, held in a private house with museum pictures on the walls, for some purpose I never fathomed or for some person whose identity I never learnt. Adrian and I were practically the only guests under thirty, certainly the only ones who looked as if we were under thirty, and we were both of us way out of our league. For all I know, my own invitation may have been a mistake, the slip-up of a social secretary who had muddled my name with someone else's. Adrian's was *not*, of course, his surname was far too well known and far too singular, but his beautiful velvety eyes, when they met mine over the buffet, seemed to imply that acceptance of the invitation had been a mistake. He was noticeably unhappy.

Nobody introduced us to one another, it was not that

sort of party, so eventually, unable to make *de jure* contact, we made it *de facto* – at least I did – by the simple method of drawing closer to him round the buffet table and spilling the contents of my plate over his sleeve.

From this undeniably sticky starting point our acquaintance took off without so much as a 'plick' of adherence and soared. Adrian's father would no doubt disagree with me, other people's trances being in his view impossible to establish or speak meaningfully about at all, but I think it is fair to say we were entranced with one another. In a trice the stiff inhospitable milieu in which we were trapped ceased to matter, ceased pretty well to exist. Amid the Braques and the cigars and the diamonds, and the bouffant Balmain gowns deployed like panzer plating, we created our own small private space and moved in it easily – occupants of a bubble car (then much in vogue) among fleets of Rollses and Daimlers. We danced and talked, and then, finding a small parking place in a corner under a Max Ernst on one side and a de Chirico on the other, we just sat and talked. First in the crude, jejune code-language of our peers designed to establish wavelength – Have you seen *La Dolce Vita*? Do you like Renoir? (Penalty if he was taken to be the painter.) Have you read *The Outsider*? (Bonus for asking which). Do you like Bach or the Romantics? Monk or Mulligan? Have you ever tried a Purple Heart? – but then, as tuning fined and the code became redundant, in a fuller, freer language, rarely used nowadays but remembered from schooldays, and in particular from school nights, when, in the company of a few invisible trusted friends, you could pour out words from your heart or head or any old where without having to check them for modishness first.

'I went to a fortune teller the other day. He says he can tell if someone's had an abortion because he sees a

bright green light, like a bog mist, over their stomach. I
don't think that's possible, do you?'

'No. No, I don't think so. I hope not, for him. Think
how awkward it'd be – on the underground and places.
Seeing green lights flashing all over the place. Would you
have an abortion, Zoë?'

'No, I don't think so, not unless I was raped or something
and absolutely hated the father's guts. But I know someone
who has.'

'You're joking.'

'No, I swear. At least I know someone who knows
someone – *extremely* well – who has.'

'Gosh.'

How nice it was to hear someone say 'Gosh' like that,
instead of acting all blasé and unshockable.

'I know.'

Silence. Leisurely, no panic about filling it up. This was
nice too.

'I know someone who died last week.'

'What, having an abortion?'

'No, silly. Just died. A friend of mine, a chap I grew up
with. He was playing tennis and kept on saying he wasn't
feeling well, and everyone thought it was because he was
losing and said what a bad sportsman he was, and then he
suddenly crumpled up and died. Right there on the court.'

It was my turn to say 'Gosh'. 'Gosh. Did you mind
about him dying?'

'No. It's crazy. I minded more about them saying he
was shamming. I was almost glad he died, just to prove
them wrong.'

'I don't think it's crazy at all, not if he was your friend.
I swallowed a safety-pin once, just because someone said
I'd never dare. But you're not glad now, are you?'

'Open?'

'What?'

'The safety-pin.'

'Yeah. Well, sort of. Bentish anyway.'

'No, I'm not glad now.'

'Was that why you were looking so sad then, over there by the buffet? Because you were thinking about him?'

'*Was* I looking sad? Was I really? Tell me what you thought when you saw me.'

'Na, na, na, not yet. I will, I promise. Later. First you tell me . . .'

Riveting stuff. We were, I think, Adrian and I, among the last to leave, and I have some vague memory not of being ousted by our hosts exactly – again it was not that sort of party, nor they assuredly those sort of people – but of being eased out of the doorway by someone professional acting on their behalf. Gently, a trifle gingerly, as if we were sleepwalkers it would be impolitic to wake.

'Can I drive you home?'

The question I had foreseen and been dreading. Yes, dreading, because I had a car. A brand-new and much-treasured powder-blue Renault Dauphine whose existence, however inconvenient, I was incapable of denying, because to do so so early on in ownership would have seemed like treachery.

Already sensing his hurt before I had caused it, I said no, and then, appalled by the pistol-shot curtness of my reply, tried to add something and floundered.

'I'm leaving, you see, tomorrow,' Adrian went on. 'That is,' and he looked up into the paling sky and down again, 'today. I won't . . . We won't . . .'

He had told me already. He was leaving to do voluntary work in Central Africa, teaching children. The fact had impressed and depressed me in equal measure, now it just depressed. I acknowledged my car by rummaging for the keys, unlocking it and getting in.

Through the window his head appeared, sideways and then, as I rolled down the glass, frontways, wonderfully close to mine. A hand shot in alongside, grasped me by the back of my beehive hairdo and pressed my face to his. Once again, as it had done with Jeremy, that strange hot-and-sweet sensation coursed through my body, using a network that was not nerve or blood vessel but seemed to run parallel to both, only deeper. This time, however, I was darned if I was going to let it mess my chances by making me behave like a twat or a twit or whatever it was I had behaved like last time. Woodenly I resisted the nuzzling lips and probing tongue, closing my teeth like a mantrap. Primly I disengaged my face from his, righted the beehive, and turned my gaze in a businesslike fashion towards the dashboard. Reluctantly, but hiding any show of reluctance under a nervous twiddle, my fingers began turning the ignition key. Twiddle, twiddle, until, with a nasty hiccup (because my clutch control was still imperfect) the Dauphine lurched forward, putting several yards between us. Kangaroo petrol, my driving instructor called it, who had learnt this and many other witticisms in the Air Force.

In the rear mirror Adrian's face was as sad as it had been before our meeting. 'Good-night then,' he called out uncertainly.

'Goodnight,' I replied. But it wasn't night, it was morning. And this wasn't the way to handle a prospective lover either but it was too late, and I was too shy, to rectify the signals. I waited a little, still hopeful of a reprieve from somewhere, until I saw him turn disconsolately on his heel, and then I lifted my foot from the pedal and bounded off into the fortunately empty streets, never to see him again. He rang later that morning but I was asleep and had forgotten to say I wanted waking, should he call. I sent him a postcard explaining this c/o the philosopher, c/o the philosopher's publishers, but I doubt it ever reached him, not in Central Africa.

AYMAR

Muffed it because I was artless and muffed it because I was artful. It seemed there was no way of hitting it right with the opposite sex, no way of achieving a balance. Getting your Man, Holding on to your Man once you'd Got him: women's magazines, the only oracles I dared consult, were full of counsels, letters, stories, articles, all of which, when you weeded out the variables, were centred on this one allegedly vital but unperformable feat. Cleopatra was said in the pages of one of them to have had an unloosenable grip on her lovers – too secret in its nature to be decently revealed – but she was an exception. Like Circe, who used magic and cheated, and Mrs Simpson, who against all odds had bagged a king. The rest of womankind, me among them – nothing but butterfingers, bad fielders, perennial pigs-in-the-middle, hopping clumsily up and down as the elusive prizes whizzed by unstopped. Why should it be so? And was it so? And need it be so even if it was? Not only did I ignore the answers to these questions, but I was too busy hopping on my own account to stop and ask them

Aymar would not elude me, however. Why should he? He needed me so much he wanted to marry me. And how could he? Thanks to a bad go of polio as a child, his right leg was eighteen centimetres shorter than his left. Added to which, or perhaps deriving from which, he was gentle. He knew about pain and was chary of inflicting it. Before he kissed me for the first time he twirled my hair around pensively for well over an hour and talked to me about Teilhard de Chardin, who he claimed was some kind of relative. The second time it was Chateaubriand – no connection. It was refreshing and seductive to be handled with such care.

I had been invited to stay with his family in their Paris flat by his parents – friends of my father's through a complicated web of connections that included the shared ownership of a racehorse: two 'legs' each. (Funny how every time I mention Aymar I am led to the subject of legs; it was the same when we were together.) The original invitation was for a specific weekend, to see the Arc de Triomphe. Which was not, of course, the monument, that it should need such careful timing, but the race, the horse race.

However, after the race, and after several days after the race, instead of being back in England again I was still there, in Aymar's flat and often as not in Aymar's arms; my invitation having been extended indefinitely by his mother, Madame la Vicomtesse, who had walked into the salon during one of our less literary moments and then walked out again, a curious, tigerish expression in her eye.

Both Aymar and I expected brakes on our movements after this discovery, but no, *au contraire*. Madame had first made for the telephone and called my parents to arrange for the extension of my stay, and then had not only left us together but had gone out of her way afterwards almost literally to throw us together on every possible occasion. Inventing one when none cropped up.

'*Allez, mes petits lapins!*' she would enjoin us, fluttering her hands and making pushing movements, ushering us into rooms, into cars, into gardens – anywhere that seemed to offer a likely cornice for our purpose. '*Allez, allez γ, amusez-vous bien!*'

Allez into the box-room to look out photographs, *allez* into the study to read poetry, *allez* to the cinema, *allez* to the Bois, *allez* to the Louvre. On one evening, when Monsieur le Vicomte was not there to raise a well-trimmed eyebrow and put down a well-shod foot, *allez* all the way to Rambouillet to listen to the stags belling in the forest. Or, in the more fleshy, less musical French version, in order to '*écouter bramer les cerfs!*'

Altogether it was a very absorbing, very rewarding stay. Now and again I would feel the Vicomtesse's eye on me, and looking up would catch her squinting at me appraisingly, like a dressmaker taking measurements. Sometimes the eye would be friendly, sometimes not; always, in the depths, there was that feline glint of warning.

I met it candidly. I loved Aymar, I knew I did, because he loved me and I was safe in his love. The rest – whether his mother thought I was a slut or an adventuress, or simply regretted, like his father did, I was not of noble birth – did not matter.

After I had left Paris we wrote to one another every day for four and a half months. (Very good for my French.) At the end of which time Aymar arrived in person, unable to bear the separation any longer. I went to fetch him from the station and took him that same evening to a party, hoping it would be a grand one and that news of it would percolate through to his parents, enhancing my commoner's status in their eyes.

Aymar's clothes were not quite right for party-going:

they had an officey look about them, and he had no dinner jacket and had to borrow one of my father's which sat on him rather ill. When I helped with his unpacking a faint smell I had never noticed before wafted out of the suitcase, reminding me of foxes. He held out his arms imploringly, but I didn't enter them, I said there was no time.

It *was* a grand party, it was a very grand one. It was held in a double marquee, lined with silk so you couldn't see the canvas, and there were two bands and two dancefloors, and flowers enough for a wedding, and scores and scores of dancers, many of whom I knew from my London launching the year before. To begin with I sat out beside Aymar at a small floorside table, holding hands with him under the cloth and shaking my head at would-be partners, but as the evening wore on I became restless and planted my elbows firmly on the table. Friends came over to talk and then sidled away again: Aymar was strong on a lot of topics besides Teilhard de Chardin and Chateaubriand – Bergson, for example; history; stamps, he knew masses about stamps – but the music was loud and English was not his language.

Under the tablecloth my feet jiggled. My impatience had little to do with dancing, and still less with Aymar's lameness, which I had considered from the outset appealing, Byronic, and still did. Nevertheless it provided me with a language and a motive for saying something I would otherwise have found impossible to say: namely that I had made a most terrible mistake in thinking that love and kindness were in any way connected. When the fifth invitation came, therefore, instead of refusing it as I had the others I leapt to my feet and allowed myself to be whirled away into the throng of dancers, leaving Aymar alone with his brace and his Gauloises and his faintly feral smell.

I danced a waltz and then a jive and then a smooch, and then changed partners on the wing and danced another suite, and another and another. My reputation for oddness usually earned me lots of gaps between partners, but tonight was different, tonight for some reason (possibly connected with game reserves and the discouraging of foreign poachers) I was in high demand. I returned only once to the table where Aymar was sitting, to find him deep in conversation with a girl I scarcely knew, and before he could switch his attention from her to me – his gentleness, as I said, was so profound it governed even his manners – I beamed at him with my flushed dancer's face and whisked off again.

We returned home at four o'clock in the morning, in silence, me driving. The next morning I slept late, and then spent a lot of time on the telephone. In the afternoon we visited the National Gallery. Fearful lest my message had not been properly received I sped through the halls as if on rollerskates, but it was unnecessary: Aymar left the very next day. For Kent, where he said he had a cousin who was studying agriculture.

I was relieved and bitterly, bitterly ashamed. The Vicomtesse's tigress eye haunted me for months, appearing behind my own when they were shut, or else flashing at me, when they were open, out of random shiny objects: buttons, jewels, once even out of a yellow traffic-light. She knew, she had known all along how it would end.

My father too, I think. But he was on my side, and his only comment on the affair was to say, when I gave him back the dinner jacket, 'Fine, Zozo, fine, but take it to the cleaner's, would you, first?'

HARRY

My father – on my side? No, incorrect, my father was not on my side, he was *against* the side my men friends were on, which meant that he was sometimes on my side, sometimes not.

After the disaster of Aymar I shied further and further away from close binary relationships with members of the opposite sex, but this didn't prevent me from seeking their company, quite the reverse. Indeed, in an acquisitive, collector's spirit, I began now to seek it quite deliberately, almost organizedly, selecting the candidates on the twin bases of amusement-value (which must be high) and sex appeal (which must be low, to prevent complications), and then strewing the elected around me like cushions, in order to brighten the surroundings.

I had an accomplice in this, or else my allure would hardly have been sufficient: a girlfriend with similar tastes, similar fears, more beauty than I – especially from the neck downwards – and a great deal more money. Each weekend, mostly at her house, which was bigger and emptier, but sometimes at mine, we would assemble around us the various pieces of our collection and hold court. I.e. we would lounge about, play the gramophone, the fool, ping-pong, tennis, backgammon, charades – anything there was to play – carry intimacy to the outer rim of flirtation but no further, and wind up, all of us, on the Saturday night by getting as drunk as we prudently dared.

Unaccountably, when it was my turn to house this costly and often rowdy circus, my parents made no objections. They required to know the names of the guests, but once these had been given and scrutinized (and, where possible, linked to some member of their own generation – Ah, yes, Teenie's boy, Whatshername's sister's son, the one that was kicked out of whereveritwas, don't you remember the fuss?), no more was said. Hospitality was an institution, like the Jockey Club: you didn't question it, you simply abided by its rules.

My mother, out of tact or boredom, it was hard to say, would usually disappear for the weekend in question, accepting some other invitation. And even when she remained technically in the house, after greeting my guests and offering them, slightly wryly, a glass of lime juice, she still contrived to disappear in much the same fashion, adducing lunch parties, dinner engagements, pressing rounds of golf. Except for breakfast, when she would again offer fruit juice to the most jaundiced and pose a few incurious questions, we hardly ever saw her.

My father also disappeared, but less thoroughly and for shorter periods. He liked it to be perceived that he was disappearing, so as to create an illusion of tolerance, and then he liked to reappear when his reappearance was least expected, to see what tolerance had spawned. It was a risky game, and therein lay its fun.

He also liked baiting, unsettling and if possible gravely embarrassing any man in whom he thought I was interested, for whatever reason. My present group foxed him a bit by its size and variability, but he was always convinced that somewhere in the midst of the jesters was a serious contender for my heart and/or head, and half the fun lay in trying to find out who he was.

The other half lay in the fight. Although fight is not quite the right word for it. My father didn't quarrel with his opponents, didn't argue, not in any recognized fashion, didn't really engage with them at all. All he did was to cast on to the surface of the conversation, one after the other, a series of patently false and kindling pronouncements along the lines of, 'All good composers were Jews,' or, 'Blacks will always be poor, they have no foresight,' or, 'Women don't enjoy the sexual act, it's the way they are made,' and then sit back, fisherman-fashion, and wait for one of his listeners to rise.

What was said, on either side, didn't interest him, and the defence of his theory, when and if he bothered to make one, would in fact be given out with a cavalier disregard for consequence: mangled quotations, snippets of poetry, anecdotes with cryptic punchlines that left the listener dizzily groping for a connecting thread – these and other ragbag oddities would be tossed insouciantly into the fray, with jerky delivery and at terrific speed. No, what interested him was watching the changes in his opponent's behaviour and trying to read things from them and construe them in as uncomplimentary a way as possible. The young man stuttered? He was gauche, and probably a fool to boot. He raised his voice? He was ill-bred, maybe even voted Labour, parents too. Not so far-fetched, when you considered the company Zoë kept nowadays. He blinked, couldn't meet the eye? Ha! Then this was probably the one. Give him a bit more rope and the fellow might obligingly hang himself. And speaking of hanging, that gave him a splendid idea for another cast . . .

I wish I had understood the motive behind this impish and often, worse, ogreish, behaviour. But then I wish a lot of things in regard to my father, chief of which that he were still alive to behave as badly as he liked. The Freudian doctrines had not made much impact on the turf-centred world in which we lived; at most some of the catchwords may have inspired the name of a racehorse: Oedipus Complex – by Royal Muddle out of Jocasta, Super-Ego – by Sir Egbert out of Selfish Miss. Not nearly enough, alas, in the way of psychological savvy to help either of us chart the undercurrents of feeling that swept us where they did, with the force they did.

Why had I loved him so blindly and so long when he was full of faults to overflowing? Our present divide was such that I had difficulty imagining. But I could remember all right that I had loved him, and the memory almost shamed me. I had cameos in my head depicting him, of a sweetness that now seemed cloying but that I knew had once been authentic, perfect. The top of his head as seen from my roosting place on his shoulders, a perch so high and privileged that no harm could reach me there. The upward journey thither in his arms – a hoist to heaven – and the asp of his tweeds and the slither of his silk shirt against my face in passing, and the smell of his shaving lotion and his specially concocted hair oil that came in fat green bottles: fascinating, distinctive, like everything else he owned. His hand with its tobacco-stained fingers that for all that were the cleanest and most wholesome I had ever seen, reaching out for mine, opening, tracing, measuring, comparing. 'See? We have the same fingertips. Spatulate, they're called. Pity for you.' (No, no, it was not a pity, it was a boon, a link, a piece of him that would be always with me.) 'Important for a girl to have pretty nails.'

I could see him standing in the parlour of my convent school, head bent, hands clasped, practising his golf address; waiting for me to come to him, unaware that I was there already. Unaware too, that that small gesture of his – that familiar flick of those familiar wrists – was sufficient to deliver me on the instant out of my prison, into another world. The real world, or so I considered it, the secular one, ripe to bursting with all the pomps and vanities the nuns were so keen for us to renounce but for which I wickedly craved. Thus in the corner of the same vignette I could see myself watching him, enchanted, feeling the ugly weight of my school fetters drop painlessly away. 'Mother Perpetual Succour says to wait for her, Daddy, she wants to talk to you – seriously – about something I did in art class.' 'Mother *What*? Say it again, Zo. Mother Perpetual Sucker? Oh my God, I can't believe it. How do you expect me to speak seriously to a person with a name like that? Come and kiss me, you evil porker, and then stand here beside me and pinch me when I giggle.' My magician, my translator, my saviour.

At some unknown point, however, and for some unknown reason, the magic had begun to grow thin (proportionately perhaps to my own growing large), and then stopped working altogether. 'Don't leap at me, Zoë, I can't catch you any more. You're not a child, you're a great big lump.' Perhaps that was when things had begun to sour.

Or maybe a little later on, when everything I did, not only leaping, appeared to offend him. 'Why can't you be more like a French girl, Zoë?' (Good question from a philosophical standpoint. Why couldn't I?) 'Why can't

you enter a room properly? Why can't you hold your
head better? Why can't you do something about your
hair/clothes/skin?'

Always questions, always accusatory, always rhetorical.
Never a practical suggestion as to how these ills – which,
God knows, bothered me just as much as they did him –
could be righted. Worse, there seemed to be an underlying
implication that to seek a solution, be it scissors or diet or
deportment lessons or simply a visit to a shop, was *ipso facto*
to forfeit whatever it was you were trying to achieve. In his
romantic vision of the world, which I longed to conform
to but couldn't, pretty girls were pretty: they didn't need
things like curlers and tweezers and acne lotion; at the
very most in the way of beauty care they could resort
to a little dab of face powder on their upturned (dratted
French again) noses and chase their already silken legs into
a pair of sheer silk stockings from dratted Paris.

But anyway, in defiance of the stricture, now I had
done something all right on these accounts. Oh yes siree.
I had stuccoed my face with vampire-white make-up, I
had ringed my eyes with kohl so as to mark where they
were in it, I had teased my hair into a column a stork
would be proud to nest on, I had learnt to enter rooms
adventurously, balancing on six-inch-high inverted knife
blades, I had docked all my hemlines to tutu-level. And
by thus doing I had gathered round myself a circle of
clever young men – yes, clever, not just quick-witted;
young, not pushing forty like some I could mention –
who admired me. Found me attractive. Liked me the way
I was. So there, carp on, I was out of earshot.

Or so I thought. But one sad Saturday evening, which
although it was many years ago I still remember clearly,
down to the dullest details I never normally noticed like

the weather (hot, drizzly, it was Wimbledon, end of first week) and the time (five to midnight), my confidence in my new-found independence took a bit of a rocking. Likewise my zest for my new persona.

I had five friends staying in the house that weekend, my beautiful girlfriend Eliza and four young men whom we had lured from their studies in the nearby university town – two of them *habitués*, two of them new.

Whetted by the newcomers my father had been at his spikiest, his most disconcerting. All during dinner, taking a most unfair advantage of his age and position as host, he had played his favourite game of cast and scarper with the four male members of the party, taunting, goading, heel-snapping, mine-laying, forcing some kind of reaction from them, be it only stupor, and then whisking himself away to some remote illogical haunt, chuckling to himself as they strove to follow.

'Don't you think, sir, that perhaps you are a little mistaken when you say it was Marx who wrote that? Couldn't it have been Malthus?'

'Tiddle iddle iddle iddle, "*Voi che sapete . . .*"' He was on to Mozart now, and apart from the 'M' there was no bridge to be seen for miles. He pronounced the 'ch' wrong too: soft when it ought to be hard. Honestly, the gaps in that man's education.

'Er . . . I mean . . . irremediable poverty is hardly a solid tenet on which to base a revolutionary doctrine of social change, which is what Marx . . .'

'Ahhh.' Big sigh and large wink at Eliza, who he adored. 'The poor are always with us.'

'Er . . . yup . . . well . . . that was sort of what we were arguing about, wasn't it, sir?'

Ruminatively, to Eliza, after a long pause. 'Sir is a very

awkward form of address, isn't it? I wonder why that should be so. Rude if you omit it, and almost ruder if you use it. *Terrible* if you repeat it. Anyone with a bit of social grace should – I don't know – sort of wriggle round the problem, don't you think?'

Eliza, in a bit of a spot. 'I dunno either. Yeah, I suppose . . . Yeah. Never really thought.'

'Girls are so much luckier in these things.' Smiling straight into her eyes. 'And so much nicer. *Always* be polite to little girls, Disraeli used to say, you never know who they will marry.'

Eliza, who had once quoted this dispiriting saying at me in disgust, attributing it to quite another source, dimpled and looked delighted. My father's courtship of her was chiefly strategic – without it he would have run the risk of appearing, not rude as he intended but quite simply mad – however, she seemed to take it as genuine homage. Probably it was that too, and probably that was why I minded.

Probably that was also why, after dinner when my father did another of his calculated disappearing tricks, leaving us to our own drunken devices, I joined so wholeheartedly in the new game which his mealtime behaviour had inspired.

It was Peter, one of the two recruits, who began it. Helping himself uninvited to a large whisky from the drawing-room drinks cupboard, he sat himself down in the armchair my father usually occupied and, twitching his rather languid frame into a position of hawklike alertness, announced in a passable imitation of my father's voice, 'The garrotte is the most humane way of inflicting the death penalty, I would say. Yes, the garrotte. Performed from behind a curtain, for choice, so as to spare the executioner's feelings.' Then he doubled up laughing.

The lure was irresistible. We all joined in, first in the

laughter and then in the game. Which quickly became a kind of contest of absurdities, as, rolling around the floor and clawing at our stomachs, we progressed from the compulsory castration of rapists, to the blinding of voyeurs, to the reintroduction of the chastity belt (subsequently turned down as invalid, because what need was there for chastity belts when women didn't like sex?), the probity of lynching, the immediate suppression of nine-tenths of the world population on humanitarian grounds, and I know not what else, all interlaced with snatches of well-known arias and completely irrelevant quotations, or rather misquotations, the triter the better.

'*J'accuse*! says Marcuse.' This was allotted two points, but only because the mimic got the pouncing gesture so absolutely right. '*Si jeunesse pouvait, si vieillesse savait.*' Weak, half a point only. 'Always be polite to little boys, you never know who's buggering them.' Good. Two and a half. Mimì to Rodolfo: 'Your tiny gland is frozen.' Three, for dirt value. '*Usque tandem*, Catherina?' Bit laboured, but give it two, seeing that it was attributed to a wilting Count Potemkin, forever on the job. '*Homo homini lupins.*' That was the one I liked best. 'Tell me, where's the fancy bread?' 'On with the mockery . . .'

Yes, on with the mockery we went, and on with the drink and on with the giggles, until someone, I think it was Peter again, got to his feet and began singing a song with my father's name in it. Not scornfully, not even unkindly, but just in a really, really loopy way, flapping his hands and knocking his knees together and then wrapping his arms round himself and hugging tight his torso, so that from the back he appeared to be in the passionate embrace of someone else. 'I'm just wild about Harry,' he warbled. 'And Harry's wild about mehe.'

It brought the house down. From my position on the floor I glanced sideways, across the other prostrate, quivering bodies, towards the rectangle of the open doorway, and in the pale midsummer darkness of the hall beyond I saw Harry standing there, still as a pointer, watching the scene.

Had he remained still I don't think I would have felt my treachery so keenly. Nor if he had moved abruptly, in anger; come forward, for example, and given us all a rocket for being so silly and so drunk – on *his* booze, moreover. But he did neither of these things. Instead, with a shy, slinking movement, utterly foreign to me, utterly foreign to himself, he drew back into the darkness and disappeared.

'Harry, Harry!' Peter was still chanting, 'Oh I am so wild about Harry!'

So was I, I realized. Still. Always was and always would be. Hell! And I rolled my head the other way and was sick over my mother's cherished *gros-point* needlework carpet.

NERI

Like Elvis Presley whose records came in very handy for this purpose, Neri may just have been another weapon to use against my father, I honestly don't know. It would be a way of explaining him . . .

Or else he may have *been* my father. A stand-in, that is to say, an effigy, a guy. Some guy.

All I know is that I saw him in a bar in Florence railway station when I arrived there on a fortnight's holiday with a couple of girlfriends, and fell in love with him on the instant. As if bewitched. Like poor Titania, only my moke was more of a dog than a moke: a thin, raffish, gipsy dog, a cross-breed, a lurcher. Goodness, he was unsavoury. I saw him once, years afterwards, queuing up in a bank in Milan (ha, a bank, isn't life dextrous sometimes?), and I was astounded. He was dirty, downtrodden, bore the stamp of the pariah, or at any rate of the individual who – maybe from choice, not necessarily because constrained to it – is somehow situated outside the fold in which the bulk of society is gathered. I heard his voice, too, when he reached the counter, and it was an outsider's voice, grating and theatrical; what Italians call, referring I suppose to musical notation, above the lines. He wheedled at the bank employee; I bet he had money troubles. Then he saw me in my cashmere polo-neck and Hermes scarf, and a startled, disoriented look flashed across his face, interrupting his spiel. I was careful to give no sign of recognition, not even a change in my breathing.

And yet, once upon a time, this shifty, stringy individual who passed himself off as a racing driver but was in fact a pimp, and a pretty unsuccessful one at that, had held the key to my heart in his hand. The heart too, for that matter. Let me see if I can remember how it happened.

The first sight I had of him was, yes, at Florence station, but I can't think I actually went up and spoke to him then, I would have been too shy. Besides, I was with my two friends, Cressida and Rosie, and I can remember that they were horrified, and did their panicky best to wipe the scales from my fast silting eyes.

'Not that one, the one in the leather jacket? You can't mean it, Zoë, he's *ghastly*. Looks like a skeleton. I've never *seen* anything so creepy!'

Cressida, in a laconic phase, simply put two fingers in her mouth and retched.

Myself, I had never seen anything so beautiful, so coveted, so immediately and magnetically attractive as this tall, thin, not so young stranger, hunched over his station *aperitivo*. I must have managed to catch his eye over the glass and convey something of my longing because we saw him again, fairly soon after our arrival, in quite another part of the city, looking as if he was looking for us, and this must have been the time that I made my move.

Again I'm not sure exactly what I did, nor in what tempo, but I trusted him so utterly that I probably made everything plain straight away. As plain as I could, that is, with my limited, bookish Italian and his harsh, aspirated Tuscan: *la hŏ'sa, la hă'sa, le hă'scine*.

I am smitten by you, Neri, I probably said, or implied by my behaviour. Do with me as you will. Take me up, indulge me, endure me, keep me by you or park me in a corner, but don't, please don't, send me away because I think I would die.

Whatever the message, it must have got through to him, because a couple of days later I was already his creature, his mascot, his amusement and (faintly but quite visibly) his encumbrance. Rosie and Cressida saw little of me. I returned to the *pensione* where we were staying, at nightime to sleep, and in daytime on quick pragmatic forays to fetch anything I needed (usually traveller's cheques), but otherwise my time was spent in my hastily constructed willow cabin at Neri's gate. Admiring, listening, aching with unwieldy love, and mostly waiting, waiting – in bars, in cars, in billiard parlours, cinema foyers, wherever I had been instructed – for the object of my love to finish whatever ill-defined commerce he was presently involved in and come to me.

Cressida, whose father was a poet, had all sorts of invitations lined up for the three of us: lunch with Sir Harold Acton to see his 'primitives', whatever they were, lunch next day with someone else to see something else, tea with Sir Osbert Sitwell. I was conscious of the honour, vaguely: 'Sirs' abroad tended to be more glamorous than you'd expect, and I had the feeling that the second one was a famous fascist politician, but how could I possibly forfeit Neri's company when it came in such tantalizingly small doses? I told Cressida and Rosie they would have to go on these jaunts alone. Which they did, cursing me for the taxi fare which worked out more expensive. 'You're dotty,' they scolded. 'Missing a free meal for that reptile.'

In fact, on account of all the waiting and hanging about, I

usually missed meals altogether. I didn't seem to need food, I just needed Neri – to be in the same room with him, to breathe in the smoke of his grassy Nazionale cigarettes, to hear the sound of his husky voice, mimicking mine, giving orders to the strange lackey figure that accompanied him everywhere, or else gabbling words I couldn't quite follow, down the mouthpiece of a telephone. That was all I required of life in my present state.

'What the hell do you talk about?' Cressida wanted (not very urgently) to know.

I thought a bit. 'About cars mostly,' I said. 'Cars. And me. He's interested in me, he asks quite a lot of questions.'

'I bet,' said Cressida and resumed her backcombing. 'You ought to try and find out more about him before he slits your throat or something. Pump that other flabby creep he goes about with.'

I loved the flabby creep too, whose name was Carlo, precisely because he was so close to Neri that some of the spell-powder had rubbed off on him. I had to admit, however, that he was very fat and wheezy and unfit, and not the best company when you had to spend as much time with him as I did.

On our next long wait, outside a second-hand car dealer's where Neri was more or less completing the purchase of a Lancia sports car to replace his Fiat 500, I did as Cressida suggested and posed a few questions. Not that I was worried about my throat, I just wanted, suddenly, to know. What did Neri do, exactly, in the way of a job? What was his surname? Where did he live? Why did he keep such strange hours? Were his parents alive? Did he have any brothers and sisters? Small basic things like that.

Carlo's doughy face, usually innocent of all expression save for a slight snoozing-dog watchfulness when Neri was around, showed genuine surprise. And then discomfort. Didn't I know? he asked, squirming his large backside on the tiny seat till it overlapped it entirely. *Veramente?* Didn't I know?

Know what? I said. I didn't know anything.

Crossly he shook his head and then, without answering any of my questions, bundled out of the car and made for the salesroom, where I saw him through the plate-glass front, talking to Neri in what was for him a very animated fashion, pointing at himself and at me sitting in the car, shaking his head again, hard, several times. I wondered, with such an ordinary set of questions, what I could have said wrong.

When they came back again to the car, which was not for a good ten minutes more, Carlo had reverted to his flaccid self but Neri seemed restless, undecided. It was, I can see that now, the stumbling block of our entire relationship: the fact that he just could not make up his mind what to do with me. A windfall of sorts had dropped into his lap, but, like a starving man with a Fabergé egg, in its present form it was of no use to him at all. The matter needed careful handling if he was not to lose out on it, and time was running short: by now there were only five days of our fortnight's holiday to go.

Later that evening, in what was possibly an attempt to seek advice, but more likely was a direct attempt to negotiate me, cash in on me, he took me to see a friend of his. A woman.

She was oldish and vanquished-looking and lived in a tiny little flat in a part of the city I had never visited, nor even seen mentioned in my guide book. I decided she must be a relation of Neri's – an elder sister maybe, or an aunt – and I took the visit as a favour and a step in the right direction. Carlo must have told him I was curious about his background, and now I was being allowed to see it. I was as friendly and polite as I could possibly be.

Not that it was easy to be either. The woman did not rise to greet me when I entered the room, merely lifted her bottom a few centimetres from the chair and then fell back again, legs ungoverned, so that I could see the hooks of her suspenders. She didn't talk much either, only '*Ah*'s and '*Si*'s and '*Ecco*'s, although you could see she was interested in me in her way because she stared long and hard, her tired, slow-moving eyes taking in every detail of my dress, from the high-piled hair to the tips of my pointed black suede shoes.

'*Carina*,' she said flatly to Neri when she had finished her scrutiny. '*Ma* . . .' And she sighed.

I had done nothing all afternoon – nothing all day, nothing really since I had arrived in Italy – and the evidence of her tiredness distressed me. The flat too, which was small and damp and bare and yet managed to contain some of the ugliest furnishings I had ever seen. Obedient to my mother's teaching that it is good to try and take people out of themselves when they are low, I began gabbling. Praising Florence (which I hadn't seen except in flashes, from the window of Neri's constantly moving car), its art treasures (ditto), the courtesy of its inhabitants (which I hadn't seen much of either, nor looked as if I would tonight), saying anything in the placatory, bead-and-bauble line that came into my mind.

But it didn't really work, or not in the manner I intended. Paola – for that is what Neri had called the woman when he introduced me – instead of coming out of herself, appeared to go deeper and deeper in, the more I chattered. Her expression, true, thanks to the retreat lost much of its initial harshness, and she summoned enough energy at one point to change her posture and set her skirt to rights, but when my inventiveness ran out and I was left facing her in silence I realized that instead of bridging the gap – already considerable – that divided us, I had widened it yet further.

She called me *Signorina* now. *La Signorina*, obliquely, not even favouring me with direct address. The distance seemed to apply to Neri too, whose hand she slapped quite viciously as it edged towards a gondola-shaped cigarette box on the little marble table beside her chair. *La Signorina* will be wanting to get back to her hotel, she told him shortly. Better take her there. She was not the sort of girl who ought to be out late at night in a foreign city.

'No?' Neri asked, placing a finger under my chin and turning my face towards him; examining it as if it were quite new to him. 'No?'

'No,' the Paola woman said, with the finality of one who had run out of patience altogether. I had demoted her fairly early on from sister to aunt, but now I began to wonder if she was even that. A relative of any degree would surely have made a titch more effort? I don't know – a few smiles, a cup of coffee, a plate of biscuits . . .

Neri seemed disappointed too by the way the visit had gone off. On the way back to the *pensione* he hardly spoke. When he stopped the car he shook his sleeve and three rather crumpled cigarettes fell out on to the seat. 'At least I got these off the old *bagascia*,' he said, and chucked me under the chin again and laughed.

So it wasn't me he was disappointed in. 'I'm sorry she didn't like me, Neri,' I said. (This was an understatement. I might have been touchy and imagined it, but I was almost certain I had heard the woman hiss after Neri as we left the flat something about him being '*pazzo*', mad, and to have nothing more to do with me. Unwarranted nastiness. Interfering bitch. I didn't know what a '*bagascia*' was but it sounded absolutely right.)

'*Beh*,' he shrugged, and then pocketed the cigarettes and leant over and kissed me. Not the preoccupied pecks he had given me so far but a proper lover's kiss. 'I like you all right,' he said. And then repeated it, as if he hadn't heard himself properly the first time.

'Like?' I said, offended. No, aghast. 'I don't *like* you, I love you.'

Again he looked at me with that strange examiner's look he had used in the flat. 'I know,' he said, making a slight puffing noise as if the fact weighed on him, which to do him justice it probably did. 'I know. And you'd do anything for me, *piccola*, wouldn't you? Anything I asked?'

I considered this large formula. Would I lie for him, steal for him, live in a flat like Paola's, forsake my parents? 'Yes,' I confirmed, 'anything.'

But my willingness only seemed to increase his burden. He threw back his head and contemplated the roof of the car, only a thumb's width above his nose, and gave a shuddering sigh that rocked the little vehicle on its axles. 'Ah, Zoway, Zoway, I could make such a fascinating woman out of you. *Hosì affascinante*. I could teach you to deal with men like this,' and he extracted one of the filched cigarettes, very crumpled by now, and twirled it around in his fingers till all the tobacco fell out. 'I could teach you how to make them think, *every* time, they are the first man you have been with.'

This was not the sort of accomplishment I aspired to. On the contrary, I wanted to exude experience, and with Neri alone, not with an entire gender. However I would have studied anything at Neri's school, even galley rowing. 'Teach me then,' I said, taking his hand with the smell of tobacco still strong on it and holding it tight against my face. Only five days left but I would *make* him love me. 'Say what you want me to do and I'll do it. Go on, try me, just say.'

He laughed and strained his head back further. 'I want . . .' he began, 'I want . . .'

'Yes?' What did he want? What could he want that he had such difficulty saying it?

'I want . . .' And then with a heavy sigh and a kind of brrrh! noise, like a horse blowing into a nosebag, he bent his head slowly forward, forward, forward, until it came to rest on the steering wheel. 'I want you to go straight back into that hotel,' he said, speaking in a sullen voice, directly into the dashboard. 'Now. Understand? Go on. *Via*! Off you go!'

'But, Neri . . .' I was lost, appalled.

'*Sciò*! *Fila*! *Fuori*! FUORI!' So angrily that, without asking any more questions, *fuori* I went.

And that was pretty much it, at least so far as the romance was concerned. While I'd been out – and the last few days I had been out almost non stop, not only as regards the *pensione*, but as regards mind, senses, everything, I was even contemplating staying on after they had left – Cressida and Rosie had been busy. Telegramming and telephoning. Even, they confessed later, going to see the Consul. They met me like a couple of Judases in the hall and broke the news to me that our parents – all six of them – wanted us back immediately. We were to leave, third class (on account of the haste and the disgrace), at daybreak the very next morning. My friends, if such I could still call them, had lost their nerve.

I turned my back on them in loathing and ran out into the street again, but it was too late. The *cinquecento*, with my nameless, addressless, numberless love inside, had gone.

'I'm going to Doney's to look for him,' I told Rosie, who had followed me and was now clinging, in a foolish, hysterical way, to my jumper. 'He's always there at night.'

She shook the jumper urgently, not letting go. 'Your father said to find out if he's asked you for money, Zo. Has he? Has he?'

Money? What did money have to do with it? I was as bewildered as if Rosie had suddenly mentioned, I don't know, Christmas stockings, asteroids, Tyrolean folksongs. Of course he'd asked me for money, that very day in fact, but only the way a friend would, because it was a Saturday and the banks were shut and he had to make an advance payment on the Lancia . . .

'Did you? Did you give him money? How much?'

Oh shut up, Rosie. Shut up! Shut up! There was something going very wrong with my chest. I felt as if I had swallowed a boiling-hot cricket ball and it was now bouncing up and down between my throat and diaphragm, pounding against each.

'You'd better ring your father, you know, just to tell him you're back. He's doing his nut.'

Again that sense of utter bewilderment. My father? Why keep mentioning my father? What use to me could he be? It wasn't my father I wanted, it was . . . Oh God, that wretched cricket ball, how much it hurt.

However, I rang my father in the end, and spluttered my heart out to him without in the least bit meaning to, and he spoke to me in return in the quiet neutral tone he had once used when he caught me on the roof of our house, walking round the parapet for a dare. 'Just catch that train tomorrow, Zo,' he said. 'Everything else can wait. We will talk about it later, OK?'

But we never did. When I got back to England the carefully neutral tone had hardened to one of frigid scorn. I wanted to ask him what had happened, whether it was possible I had loved this man who everyone was now so horrified by, including myself, and if not love, what it was I had felt for him. But the one time I summoned up enough courage to broach the topic he sprang away like a chamois. 'Love!' He spat fastidiously into his pink gin. 'Spare me the Shirley Temple act. What did love have to do with it?'

Precisely.

LEANDER

There is no story here, just a painting. No, not even that: paintings have shapes and borders and are entities, things in their own right. What follows is more a frieze of washy brush-sketches, colours running into one another, edges sometimes overlapping, sometimes not touching at all. There is no shape, you see, because there was no shape, and that is the whole point.

Me stepping into a lift, alone, on my way – I don't know where, perhaps to a museum, a lunch party, a dentist – and stepping out of it in the company of a young man, who in the space of the four-floor ride has suddenly become very important to me, and vice versa.

Me sitting in the radius of a telephone reading a book. Not just pretending to myself or others I am reading, but actually reading. I can do this now: the telephone rings punctually; instead of an instrument of torture it has become a friendly and useful object. On the other end it is (nearly) always him. Eliza calls him my swain and is pleasingly jealous.

Me at home, brushing the dogs. 'You haven't done that for a long time,' says my father in passing. He still fights shy of me as if I were a leper, but things like this ruffle his certainties. Perhaps I am not a criminal nymphomaniac, perhaps I will turn out all right after all.

The young man – Leander – in a corduroy jacket the colour of honey, flicking back his straight floppy hair from his forehead and telling me, bubbles forming slightly in the corners of his mouth, he loves me. And this news causing inside me, not, as I had always imagined it would, satisfaction, still less triumph, but concern: for the first time in my life a man, practically a stranger, for it is only a month since our meeting in the lift, has managed to touch that well-hidden, unmarked spot where my feelings are situated. I do not love Leander back, not yet, but I sense that it is possible I may do, will do. It is a curious experience, without precedent. Deliberately, like a scientist making an experiment, I say something cutting in return; not to hurt him for the sake of hurting, but to see if in hurting him I hurt myself.

Which I do. The spectre of Neri, already fading fast (and even faster since the receipt of a joke telegram from Cressida scaring the wits out of me, worded in macaronic Italian: 'Awaita me, *amore*, I arrive your country tomorro. *Baci*. Neri.'); the spectre of Neri, then, or what is left of it, melts harmlessly away, leaving just a little dry ring of rue. What a dolt I was, but it looks as if life is not going to punish me on that account; on the contrary, in the person of this dear, interesting, interested being who wants to spend all his available time with me, and I with him, it is sending me a reward.

Eliza's house, and another of our collectors' evenings, which have become *her* collector's evenings now: my collecting days being to all practical purposes over. Her parents are away and we are high as buzzards. Leander is away too;

he is conscientious about his family and has to spend time with them – just a little, now and then. Eliza, who doesn't quite get on with him, not as well as I would like, has taken advantage of his absence to draw me back into her circle. 'You must come, Zoz. You can't not. Everyone's coming. We've got the whole house to ourselves, we're gonna get stinkers.' And so we have. In Eliza's household there is a butler, and the sole mechanism of restraint is activated by the appearance, every half-hour or so, of this courteous, professional man, carrying out his duties in the face of our foolish anarchy. However, we have now reached the stage where we scarcely notice him, where his sobriety no longer checks us, and very soon we will go one step further, no doubt, and begin to find it funny. Julian, one of the waggiest wags, has already tried to draw him into the conversation and been elegantly rebuffed. No one has been sick yet, but when they are it will be the signal for more licence. Vomit is like that in this group, it acts as a kind of fanfare.

Eliza herself is the first to succumb, but seeing as it's her house she has the adroitness to plunge towards the hall and just make it to one of the hydrangea pots flanking the front door.

'Whadderwe do this for?' she asks between retches.

I am too groggy to reply, but privately I think in my case it is because I am weak. A born follower. I don't even like alcohol. There used to be a reason, connected to some current, some exasperating eddy that churned away inside me and that drink seemed to still, but now I have Leander and the cure is no longer needed. Lucky he's not here to see me.

And yet suddenly he is. He has abandoned his family in my honour and has driven all the way to where he knows he will find me, and is standing in the doorway, his trousers only a foot from Eliza's improvised basin.

We are physically awkward with one another still, almost inept, and I intend to use my drunkenness as a means of propulsion, washing us over the hurdle of sex on a swell of liquor, in fact sweeping the hurdle itself clean away, but it doesn't work like that when we try it. Probably, I tell myself, because Leander has so much ground to make up that our elevation doesn't match: I am soaring when he is low, and when he finally makes quota, I am over the top and plummeting fast. We chase each other like that for the best part of the night, never quite meeting, and in the early hours of the morning fall asleep in one of the many spare bedrooms, enervated, in each other's arms. In the morning we laugh about what has happened – or hasn't happened – between us. We are so close we can say anything to each other, and we know this silly little technical matter will not prise us apart one inch.

My house on a quiet Sunday evening, after Leander, my only guest for many weekends now, has departed. My father sits staring into the fire, twiddling a tuft of his hair. Every now and then he seems on the point of saying something, but each time I raise my eyes in expectancy he huffs and scrutinizes another part of the blaze. He approves, I know he approves, but I am anxious to see what form his approval will take. Never know, could be rage. Eventually and with great suddenness he wheels round to face me. 'At least he is a gentleman,' he says. And then leaps up and flees the room. I have to chip hard at the formal façade of the comment before I see the depth of generosity that lies behind. Grudgingly, but he has bestowed on a major rival his major accolade.

Days, weeks, months of highly strung happiness. Fountains of words and ideas always playing. So much to communicate to one another that our voices, Leander's and mine, overlap almost continuously, even over the telephone, where it is more difficult to untwine the strands. So much to laugh about that my puritanical streak, which used to classify some topics as unfunny a priori, is squeezed out of existence. Our friends watch us, not always benignly: we have a few in common, but most – and this is strange – are separate, either mine or his.

This doesn't matter to us, willy-nilly we roll them all together: love me, love my love. We like to be surrounded by people, be they friends or cinema audiences or fellow diners in a restaurant, because, alas and annoyingly and inexplicably, the wretched sex hurdle is still standing, and the only times we are not entirely happy in each other's company are the times we are alone, *à deux*, clearing it, or trying to.

Still life, this one. Vanitas with ashes. Leander's digs at university. A rented room on the outskirts of the city, in a little pebbled house you can only apply the description 'modest' to. It is indeed the modestest house I have ever been into for any length of time. Its landlady is modest too and shuns discovering us, to the point of hiding we know not where when we enter. It has an air, therefore, of being empty and neglected. It is a sad house and the room is a sad room. The overall colour – walls, carpet, bedspread, all contribute to it and all partake in the result – is tortoiseshell. As worn by a tortoise. The smell is must. There is a gas fire and a sofa and a bed and a kettle: the basic set of objects that not even a bailiff is allowed to remove. And if you except the soft furnishings, which you more or less have to, so blatantly transient are they, there is nothing else of any permanence.

In the space between the fire and the sofa, narrow on account of the cold, lie our clothes, Leander's and mine, two half-empty tea-cups, an overflowing ashtray, several unread books and several crumpled-up tissues. I have observed this scene so steadily, not caring to look elsewhere, that my memory is Pelmanized. The books are law books: law being the subject that Leander is (not) reading for his degree. His finals are coming up shortly and his parents are beginning to look on me, when I visit his home, with a growing air of resentment. They see me as an obstacle to their son's achievement, and they are right, I am. I wish I wasn't, I would do anything not to be, but I am, I am, to my deep shame I am. The clothes are only the outer ones: we have decided to avoid nakedness for a while: it is, as its companion adjective suggests, too stark. The teacups contain not tea but whisky.

A party in a house rather like the above, only bigger and fuller and noisier. A girl who looks just like me (but cannot be, surely?), behaving in a loud, attention-claiming way, laughing like a jackass and kicking off her shoes and dancing with lots of different partners, flirting hectically with each. A man who looks slightly different from the Leander of six months earlier – thinner, crosser, drunker – sitting in a chair in a corner of the room, talking studiedly to someone else, refusing to notice.

Myself in yet another room on these lines, lying naked on an unmade bed, waiting for someone who neither looks like nor is Leander to come out of the bathroom and make love to me. Leander knows I am there, and knows why I am there: I do too, theoretically, but it feels as if I have forgotten. I do not want this experience which I have conned myself into thinking will make a break between us, I long only for Leander.

The bathroom door opens and I prepare to face my ordeal, but instead of the person I am expecting, a strangely dressed figure emerges with a whip in one hand and a mackintosh in the other, and with extreme punctiliousness begs me to get up off the bed, don the mackintosh, belt it tight, and strike him with as much force as I can muster. I have picked a weirdo. Just as punctiliously I decline, get out of the place as fast as I can, and rush to Leander to tell him all about it. We make cocoa, I spend the night with him, and every now and then the bed is shaken by one or other of us giggling.

The fortune teller's. (Which just shows how muddled I am. I proclaim myself a materialist, never go near a church, equate the supernatural with superstition and superstition with bunk, how in the world do I think a fortune teller can be of any help? And yet it is the second time I have consulted him. Must be, like Freud said, the fact that when advice costs money it is valued accordingly. In this case to the extent of fifteen quid.) The fortune teller, Mr Noble, is feeding his cats. Dispensing nourishment and, I hope, wisdom at the same time. 'This young man you are presently involved with – understand me well: I am not advising you to marry him.'

The formula strikes me as a trifle weak. 'Does that mean you are advising me *not* to marry him?'

Cat food sprays as he vigorously shakes the feeding spoon. 'Cluck, cluck. It means what it says, young lady: that I am not advising you to marry him.'

But I need more direction than that. 'You're not dancing a hornpipe either.'

'Pardon?'

'Should I marry him or shouldn't I? He wants me to. I want me too.'

There must be some professional or even legal stricture on a clairvoyant's giving straightforward advice to a client. Perhaps Mr Noble thinks I am a stoolie, sent to trap him. Tetchily and to my mind somewhat mulishly he repeats, three or four times so that there can be no mistake, 'I am not advising you to marry him.'

And there, on a negative assertion as limp as a dishcloth, goes my weekly allowance.

The interior of a hugely dark and hugely expensive restaurant. Leander's advice, whispered across candles and Tournedos Rossini, is costlier and much, much stronger. 'Marry me,' he pleads. 'It'll work out. We are made for one another. Don't let . . .' We have stopped referring to our trouble explicitly, and this is perhaps a mistake: unnamed, it seems to gain in menace. 'Don't let anything cause you to doubt that, even for a minute. You'll never find anyone so right for you as I am, anyone who will love you half so much or understand you so well or make you laugh so much or – I don't know – just offer you the sort of life you want to lead. You know that, don't you?'

The sad thing is that I do. Absolutely. I know that all what I have been taught to regard as my higher functions will be safer and better tended in Leander's hands than in those of anyone else I am likely to meet. Ever. He will feed my brain for me, cosset my imagination, give doses of tonic to the artist in me, bring breakfast in bed to my sense of humour. If I have a soul he will care for that too.

In his company I will not grow mean or sluggish or dull or introspective: he is a scourer of the spirit, he will polish the windows of my mind and make sure that the furniture inside is always dusted, pushing it around when necessary, adding new pieces, persuading me to throw the old ones away.

Knowing all this, and wanting all this, why is it that I shake my head in the expensive darkness and deliver what is to both of us a death blow? I feel like the owner of an aviary who has sacrificed all his beautiful birds for the sake of a sow he keeps in the cellar.

'I think I'm going away for a while,' I say. 'Back to Italy.'

'Where you will let dozens of randy Italians make love to you.' His voice is so bitter it curdles me to anger.

'Perhaps. If I feel that way inclined.'

Oh yes, you'll feel that way inclined all right, is what his tone implies, but the words he actually speaks are different.

'Hell,' he says. 'Blast, I've come without my blasted wallet.'

'Give them a cheque.'

But we have overstretched ourselves in coming to this particular place and a humiliating scene ensues in which the waiter, and then the head waiter and then the manager, refuse with escalating snootiness what they evidently consider this dicey form of payment. We drop names but they fall unfielded, unbelieved.

'My uncle is a regular customer of yours,' Leander tries.

'Good,' comes the stony reply. 'Excellent. Cash please, sir, if you do not mind.' Eventually I burrow into my Chelsea holdall and emerge a full minute later, hair awry, with just enough notes almost but not quite to cover the bill, minus coffee, minus tips.

We are too young and too skint to stage our dramas properly, thus our last *adieux* take place on the pavement outside the restaurant, under the scornful eye of the untipped doorman, who has probably been told to scan us for stowed-away ashtrays and other plunder.

Leander insists on writing out a cheque – to me this time, to cover the expense of the meal; our last supper. All his emotion seems to funnel itself into the execution of this task: finding a pen, getting it to work, hopping around on one leg while balancing the cheque book on his other knee, and then filling in the appropriate blanks in a legible hand in the rainy semi-darkness. All mine goes into trying to dissuade and/or impede him.

We scuffle around under shelter of the awning, battling over this small piece of paper, for what seems even to us an inelegant length of time, bordering on the grotesque, but we are too worked up to care about appearances. At one point we trespass too close to the fringe of the awning and receive a soaking and the cheque has to be scrapped, but it is not victory because Leander immediately embarks on another one, which again I try to scupper in the same manner, manoeuvring him into the wet while he is off balance.

Slowly, without our realizing it, the foyer of the restaurant fills with people: other diners, waiters, even the snooty *Maître* and snootier Manager, all come to watch our ballet. When finally I give in and accept the second, or maybe it is third mushy cheque, and stuff it defeatedly into my holdall while Leander executes a kind of exultant Flamenco heel-stamp, there is a round of applause from the onlookers and then a burst of laughter. We are not invited back into the restaurant, that would clearly be unwise, but we are granted a public shriving on the threshold. The loo-lady emerges from her bower, scented towel in hand, and mops my hair for me, the Manager in person hands us two glasses of cognac on the house, and offers to lend us the taxi fare. Quite why I don't know, but our *pas de deux* has evidently convinced him of the basic solidity of our finances.

'You will repay me,' he says, brimming with sudden *bonhomie*, 'ze next time.'

'There won't be a next time,' Leander says, dipping his head in my direction. 'She's leaving me. For ever.'

A shocked 'Ooooh!' reverberates round the assembly. The Manager drops his French accent and looks genuinely concerned. 'Ask her to marry you then,' he advises. 'That usually does the trick.'

'I have. Just now. This evening.'

'And she turned you down?'

Another 'Ooooh', a muted one this time, follows on Leander's nod, and then a buzz of chatter. Guests and staff are taking sides, putting forward opinions. I think in admiration what a talent Leander has for social embellishment, for turning dull or trivial incidents into fully fledged events, for glazing things, arranging them in a pattern. I also think what wonderful copy it will give us for giggling over afterwards, but only briefly, before I realize my mistake.

Alone, in the underground, on the way back to the London flat in which I am staying, I extract the fought-over cheque from my bag and see that Leander has written out the sum as, 'Thirty-two pounds with love.' I tell myself that the day I cash it in I will know I am cured of my love for him, but for some reason – whim, regret, or simply the fear of arousing merriment in the cashier of the small provincial branch with which I bank – I never do.

MICHAEL

One figure ran in and out of my life like a thread: Michael. He had been a page at my parents' wedding, so the thread stretched beyond my life really, taking up its weaving motion before the fabric proper had commenced.

He was nearly always there, somewhere discreet and lateral, near the selvage. Or else he cropped up centrally, but on the reverse side, so that he never really figured in the pattern. I knew much more about him than he did about me, and was much more aware of his progress than he was of mine. Indeed it is probable that, beyond my name and parentage and the capacity to recognize me in a police line-up, had this ever been required, he knew nothing about me at all.

He was Irish and stunningly good-looking, with shiny black hair that never trespassed into greasiness, and long, soft Tartar eyes, and a bluish bloom to the jawbone that comes from really rebellious beard-growth (yum), and had the reputation – entirely positive in the mouths of those who voiced it – of being a bit wild.

I was at school with a second cousin of his, a certain Ginny, as besotted about him in her unnoticed way as I was myself, only with more opportunities for observation, and she was my chief source of information regarding him. She was also the point of sporadic contact, inasmuch as she would sometimes invite me to her nearby house for weekends, where it was possible (although only just, because the kinship was a loose one and his visits were rare) to catch a glimpse of this mythical Michael dashing up the staircase to change from one set of sports clothes to another, or gobbling something out of hours in the kitchen, watched over by an adoring cook, or else stretched out flat on a sofa, his face buried in cushions, recuperating from some much canvassed excess the night before.

When we were eleven, and still firmly in junior school, Ginny and I had the luck to go down with the chicken pox – together, like skittles – on one of these weekends, and during the period of convalescence we were able to tot up the record sum of five different Michael sightings: two overhead ones of him parking his car and walking all the way down the path to the front door; one (brief but garnished with 'Hello theres', and 'How's it goings', and 'Lor, you look a sight, the pair of you!') in the corridor on the way to the bathroom; one much longer one, when the scabs were off and we allowed downstairs, of him prowling round the study, waiting for some girl to turn up who he was taking to the cinema; and one final one, the best, of him coming out in the rain to say goodbye, and tucking us up in rugs in the back of the car, and winking at us and calling us Women, and telling us to Jazz up those old nuns a bit and tell them from him they must let us out more often.

We needed these sightings like Lourdes needs the odd miracle, to convince us, through the long dull men-free terms ahead, we hadn't just invented our idol out of wishful thinking. But after the bonanza of the chicken

pox we were sadly granted very few, and had to be content
with second- and often third-hand reports. Fourth-hand for
me, by the time they reached me from Ginny: Michael's
not bothering with university, he's going straight into the
bloodstock business. My mother says in her letter that
Michael's bust his collar bone/left his girlfriend/going on
a trip to Greece/taken up with someone else. She says Aunt
Cath's worried/furious/worried/furious and the new one's
not a patch on the last.

Aged thirteen and a bit our luck took a brief turn and
we were treated, not to Michael himself, who was off
buying mares somewhere for his bloodstock enterprise,
but to a whole afternoon in the company of the current
girlfriend. Which, given the boundless, hopeless character
of our admiration, we considered almost as good. After all,
through her we could learn all sorts of private things about
him that would keep us going for months: what kind of
toothpaste he used (so that we could use the same), whether
he still had the same car (so that we could look out for it,
or one like it, wherever we went), where he was spending
Christmas, how long he was staying in England this time,
how long it would be again before he was back.

If either of us had had any tiny unconfessed ambitions
towards gaining a foothold in Michael's heart (and the
Cinderella syndrome was deeply rooted in both), the
girlfriend put the lid on them. A Brueghel peasant might
as well hope to switch canvas and hop into a Fragonard
– we being the peasants and she being the Fragonard.
Goodness, she was beautiful. Her name was Joanna.

Ginny and I were edging into make-up by then, applying
wobbly daubs of the stuff to our faces in the back of
the car the moment it had passed the convent gates,
but Joanna, although five calendar years older and five

light years more sophisticated, wore none. We were into fashion too: pencil skirts, fishnet stockings, fluffy twinsets, high-perched Bardot scarves worn over a dummy bump on the crown, giving a Frankenstein elongation to the head. Joanna wore a simple corduroy dress, belted in at her eighteen-inch waist. Her mid-length hair hung straight and flat and swayed like a child's when she moved. (Whereas ours, curse those *Woman's Own* beauty hints, was stuck fast with lacquer.) She wore lightweight moccasins with flat heels. For which she even had the grace to apologize, saying that she loved shoes like ours but couldn't wear them on account of her height.

She was kind, she was tactful, she was shining, she was perfect, and to crown the perfection in our eyes she was just a teeny bit sad: loving Michael (didn't we know it) involved a lot of forbearance.

The next year, still no Michael, and no girlfriend either, but during the summer-term break we were given a closer insight into the cause of Joanna's sadness. The present cause, that is; there had allegedly been others. Ginny's mother had a female cousin staying in the house – not Michael's mother, luckily, who would probably have been less well informed, but a sister of the same, much younger, practically the same age as *You Know Who* – and the two women spent the whole weekend, which was a long one, Friday to Tuesday, discussing the recent, dramatic development in Michael's love life. He was having an affair with an Older Woman. Indeed he was having what the two cousins called, with no apparent censure for either party, a rip-roaring affair. Good for him. Good for her. She's a great goer, always was, had her eye on him for ages and can you blame her? Their voices tended to drop a bit when names were mentioned, and to slur over a few interesting details, like what 'poor old Wurrawurra' had said when he found out about it, and how 'Brrm Psst' had come across the lovers sneaking up the stairs of the Connaught Hotel together and that was how it all got out, but otherwise they made no attempt at concealment, considering us, I suppose, either too young or too green, or simply too out of the picture, shut up as we were in our convent, for it to matter.

The OW's exact identity we did not discover, only her Christian name, Elizabeth, which was so ordinary it was not much help, but we learnt that she was the wife of someone very, very important in the horse-racing world. A leading figure, worse, a power. Poor old Wurrawurra, that is, was not poor at all, but vastly rich, the owner of a whole string of race horses, a bigwig in the Thoroughbred Breeders' Association, a baronet, a Steward of the Jockey Club to boot (boot fits rather nicely there), and somebody therefore able to affect Michael's chances in a decidedly negative way, should he, Wurrawuura, be so unsportsmanlike as to take the thing amiss.

At present, however, the thing seemed to be not amiss but fine, just fine. In best equine tradition, traces were being kicked, oats were being sown, the fast-movers were going a spanking pace and looking behind their bridles, but very soon, you could bet your breeches, they would slow down again of their own accord and trot back obediently into their stables and nobody would be any the worse for it.

That was how our elders saw it anyway. Ginny and I tended to take a different view. Differing also among ourselves – she forgiving, I less so – but agreeing on the fundamental and very sobering point that on us and our hopes it was another lid. A heavy, tight-fitting one this time, like the plate-caps on an Aga range. With Joanna the fantasy element at least had remained alive: if we couldn't *be* her, on the receiving end of Michael's attentions, we could still imagine what it felt like to be in her pretty flat shoes, we could connect, we could transpose, we could shut our eyes and dream. But with this dashing and relentless predatrix of many summers this was no longer possible. How could you switch yourself, even for dreaming purposes, into a celebrated 'great goer' of your mother's generation? The gap was specific, no, wider, generic; it could not be bridged.

So that was it, and the dream Michael was dead, killed like Devereux by the cruel Elizabeth. But the real Michael kept weaving his way through my life nevertheless, marginally, the way he always had.

That winter, in my own home where the matter was discussed also, I heard more talk of him. Less sanguine this time round, more melancholy. No longer lucky Michael but poor Michael, and no longer naughty Elizabeth but silly Elizabeth. Almost patronizing, this last epithet, stressing the age factor: silly *old* Elizabeth. What does she think she's up to, making such a fool of herself? She ought to know better. So sad for Wurrawurra. And he's been so good about it too. So harmful for Michael, and so *difficult*. Hurling herself on him like that . . . what on earth does she expect him to do? It's not as if he could ever marry her or anything, the whole thing is just too ridiculous.

From hatred of her mysterious Ladyship I passed, briefly, almost to compassion. Until – it must have been another six months or so, maybe more – a large and beautifully embossed invitation arrived for my parents, summoning them to Michael's wedding.

The text implied no Vronsky nonsense though, no leavings, no scandals, no divorcings: Michael had begun a clean sheet and was marrying an heiress, Irish like himself,

Catholic like himself, dotty, so everyone said delightedly, about horses. Not a beauty – I saw the photographs afterwards in the *Tatler* – but young, attractive, serious-looking, with a kind and slightly mischievous smile. She looked nice, and I felt mean about hating her the way I did.

Later still, when I was seventeen or thereabouts, old enough anyway to frequent such places, I saw both of them in a nightclub. She, the nice-looking wife, was sitting at a table talking to a red-faced man, very ugly, putting what was clearly a certain amount of effort into the task, and he, Michael, was dancing. With someone neither red-faced nor ugly, I may add, and without any discernible effort at all.

All the old aspirations, stifled so long under the Aga lid, flared up again as my eyes met his over the partner's shoulder and I saw his chin tilt upwards in minimal sign of recognition. I was not a schoolchild any more, I was fledged, female, part of his world, and as such he would surely see me. Really see me, not for the tenth or twelfth or twentieth time or whatever the count amounted to, but for the first.

However, 'Hi there, seen Ginny lately?' was all he said to me when at last, after much careful navigation, I managed to edge close to him on the dancefloor. 'Great girl, Ginny.'

Yeah, great girl, Ginny, and great fool, me. Back into the compressor went the hopes and on went the lid, and on went the weft of my life, chasing the Michael strand further and further into the border and finally engulfing it or dropping it altogether.

Not cutting it though, that didn't happen for another few years still. A couple of weeks after the break-up with Leander I was invited to a dinner party by some married friends, slightly older than myself, where I was placed next to a jowly puce-faced man of few words and fewer thoughts who paid a certain amount of clumsy attention to me, extending uninviting invitations to various horsy venues and pressing me for my telephone number, which I carefully neglected to give. The main course was rump steak, and the *clou* of his courtship consisted in his prodding the meat on my plate with his fork and remarking on my 'nice little rump'. Was it rare? Was it tender? Was it juicy? Certainly looked it. Wished he could have a bite.

He got a lot of mileage out of this idea and everyone else, me foremost, a lot of embarrassment. In proportion to the mileage.

Afterwards my friends apologized about the evening, attributing their guest's behaviour to loneliness after his recent divorce and giving me a bit of his life story – a sequence of failures, all very sad, had been scrumptious once though you wouldn't think it to look at him now – and it was then that I made the connection: Michael at last. An overdue, overblown, overripe Michael, mine for the picking.

ELIZA

I rather liked that brush-sketch method I used for Leander, I think for Eliza I will go back to it. Accuracy without exertion. Only in this case, out of nostalgia for a time when this book was bible, compass, talisman, machete, everything to us, even badge of our own silliness, I will number the paragraphs and sub-paragraphs progressively, like those in Wittgenstein's *Tractatus*.

1. Unremembered but clearly documented by a photograph that scares me, so ancient it now looks: Eliza and I propped in sitting position in the two far corners of a play-pen, north-east and north-west, both looking bored and hostile, if this is a viable combination. Eliza is already better shaped and better dressed. My eyes, however, are glintier and my head seems firmer on my shoulders; Eliza's has a definite loll.

2. A tennis court in the huge grounds of Eliza's house and two skinny figures, hers and mine, listlessly scooping a ball down it at one another, clop, clop, clop. We have been enjoined by our parents, on this as on many other occasions, to

'play' with one another, and this is the only game that allows us to carry out the injunction while conserving a sense of autonomy. We will go through the ludic motions all right but we are blowed if we will really what *we* call play.

2.1 Ditto on a rainy day, *mutatis mutandis*, with the court a table and the game a jigsaw puzzle and me doing the sky and Eliza the toadstools in the foreground, so that contact is avoided altogether. However this passive rebellion itself is beginning to grow into a bond of sorts: something, to our mutual disgust, is building up between us. Better make sure it is a wall.

2.2. Some years on. Yet more tennis, but a foursome this time, with two of Eliza's cousins. She has cousins like I have spots: dozens of the brutes. All athletic, all self-assured, all with sonorous names that would crush a lesser being, like Hermes and Tacitus and Ça Ira, complete with cedilla. I try to look down on the lot of them but they are so tall and glamorous it is not easy. When they are together in more than two they speak backwards – 'sdrawkcab' – and I am too slow-witted to join in, bar the occasional 'on' and 'sey'and 'I wonk', which are really feebler than silence.

2.2.1. I sweat and stutter and flounder and try to ape the other players' poise, but I am outclassed on every front and it is clearly Eliza's victory. She has no trouble speaking to me, is in fact rather kind and chatty for a change. 'Come again soon, Zoz,' she chirps, knowing darn well I won't if I can help it. 'It was such fun.'

2.2.2 In the car on the way back my father, who must

have noticed my drubbing, makes matters worse by suggesting that perhaps I ought to change schools and go to the one Eliza attends. Nuns are all very well when you're small, he says, but now that I'm older a bit more – what should he call it? – finesse wouldn't come amiss. Eliza is enchanting, so grown up and yet so natural. Wonderful too with old fogies like himself. Did I notice the way she left all her friends in the middle of the game just to come over and . . .? I did, the greasy flirt. I nip this loathsome idea of co-education in the bud by reminding him high-mindedly that Eliza attends a Protestant establishment which it would be sinful for me to frequent. I've got him here and he knows it: his fault for having me so well catechized. Ah yes, of course, sin. Well, never mind, it was just a thought.

3. My arrival some years later in just such a sinful school (if school you can call it), in Oxford, where I am to study languages in the company of five privileged fluff-brains like myself, under the direction of an unqualified Russian tart – white, retired – whom our several parents have somewhat adventitiously decided is an expert in the field. I enter the bedroom I am to share with an unknown companion for the next six months to find Eliza, already unpacked, sitting on the biggest and softest bed, strumming on a guitar. We blink at one another like owls and our feathers ruffle, but there is nothing to be done; we are caged. 'You know the talented Eliza, Zoë?' the tart asks, who is standing behind me and is evidently good at picking up vibrations. Good

at buttering up her richer pupils too: the noise
Eliza is clawing out of the guitar is atrocious. I
nod. The woman turns me round and places a
decidedly unbuttery finger on my nose. 'We say
"*Oui, Madame*" here.' But I am speechless in my
dismay and can do no more than nod again.

3.1.   The same room two months later. Eliza is still in
possession of the best bed, but only for sleeping;
in the daytime it belongs to both of us. We lie
on it now, head to tail like sardines, cloaked in a
nimbus of cigarette smoke and little else. We are
doing our nails and homework at the same time.
Eliza is also, at intervals, reading out loud a letter
from her mother that has recently arrived. It is
a sharp, censorious letter and this surprises me:
until now I had always imagined Eliza's family
life to be perfect, like everything else that touches
her. 'What do you mean, a London season is a
waste of time?' she reads, tapping contemptuous
ash over the letter and emphasizing its sharpness
by giving no expression whatever to her voice.
'Who are you to judge? And what is all this
sudden passion for higher education? If you had
really wanted to go to university, you would have
thought of it earlier and taken your A levels in
time like your cousin Melissa. You say your mind
is made up, but quite honestly I don't believe it,
any more than I did over the modelling or the
acting school or the leper colony. How can I?
Only a short while ago you were writing to me
in horror that you had to share a room with Zoë,
your *bête noire* of always, and now, in your latest
letter, it transpires that she has meanwhile turned

into your greatest and dearest friend. What is this if not yet another instance . . .?'

3.1.1. The letter goes on and so, fitfully, does the reading and the grooming and the study, but I find it difficult to pay attention to any of these things any more. I am too darn happy. I keep jolting Eliza's elbow with my foot with its varnished nails and cotton-wool buffers and crooning, to the tune of a French song that fits the words beautifully, '*Bête noire, bête noire de mon enfance.*' She has written to her mother about me, she has put her soul on paper: it is safe at last, not to love her because I have done that since God knows when, probably since the play-pen, but to let my love out of its wrappings.

3.2. A portrait. Girl on a bed. Eliza is strictly speaking brown, practically all over apart from her teeth and her eyewhites, but not with the brown I have been taught to place before study or Windsor or paper, and to associate with dullness, uniformity; on the contrary, her brown is protean and brilliant and ranges from the palest fawn of her skin, to the copper of her hair, to the russet of her lips and the caramelled sugar of her irises, through to the darkest tones of all, the near ebony of her pubic hair and the near carbon of her one damaged toenail, crushed to this hue by a pony when she was eight. When, a tragically small number of years later, I am to read of her death in a three-day-old newspaper in a foreign country, I shall be unable to believe what I read, even though there is a photograph of her that takes up half the page with her name underneath, until I come across the words of a bystander who is reported as having seen 'a little brown arm sticking out of the wreckage, holding a prayer book'. I shall not know what to make of the little, still less the prayer book which I imagine was Wittgenstein again, or else a dictionary, but the brown will tell me – worse, scream out of the page at me – that it is indeed Eliza and that henceforth I am on my own.

3.2.1. Back to the bed again: it is, like the poet Donne says (we are keen on Donne because he is so randy), our centre. Our centre of communications, operations, everything, even balance. Our parents think we are learning foreign languages; Eliza and I think – rather differently because we have discovered Oxford has other things to offer in the way of study – we are learning about life, sex, men, drink, existentialism's impact on our wardrobe and amphetamines' impact on us, just to mention a few items on our secret curriculum. Whereas what we are really doing, as we lie here night after night with the door closed on the other boarders, combing through the transgressions of the day, is learning about each other. We ask the regular, 'What did he do?' time and time over, but, the answer proving much the same, it is the subsequent, 'And what did *you* do?' that engrosses us more. Because therein lies the measure of our nerve, the cast of our morals, the nature of our beliefs, the strength of our loyalties, vanities, appetites, in fact everything about one another we most crave to know.

3.2.2 I'm not sure what Eliza's discoveries are – mostly,

I think, they will concern my trustworthiness which she probably doubted before and has since found out is absolute, now she is my friend. Also, to some extent, my stability, which is likewise much greater than it looks: I appear to be a skimmer, in fact I am a plodder. If she is hyper-observant she may also have noticed that I have a very pagan frame of mind for a Catholic and a very Lutheran conscience for a pagan. And that'll be about it. On my side I learn, slightly to my pique but mostly to my undying admiration, that Eliza is without exception the best and bravest person I have ever met. She is frightened, far more so than I am, of making new experiences, but she goes for them flat out and crams them, one after another, into her baggage. She has touched a male member in state of full erection, with her bare fingers, without trousers or hankies or anything in between. (Describing it afterwards in infuriatingly hermetic terms as being just like a cauliflower, and refusing to elaborate.) She has spent a night out of school, playing poker for reefers, and vice versa has smuggled a malleable undergraduate into our room to spend the night with us. A terrifying experiment, because he snored all the time, and when he didn't snore he chortled. Bravest of all − so brave I have since been told by doctors it is impossible and that I must have imagined it, although I know otherwise − she has inserted a trial tampax into her urethra instead of her vagina, and, egged on by an unsympathetic me, has got it to travel a good three-quarters of an inch before she realizes her mistake. In our *modus operandi*, you see, we are like a trapeze duo: she doing the plunging and leaping and twirling, and I standing on the relative safety of the platform, catching and counting and throwing the ropes.

4. Portfolio of miscellaneous sketches, meriting only a quick flick through because I have shown most of them before. Two disgruntled débutantes yielding to parental pressure and doing the rounds of the London season; bumping into each other often – and often literally – on staircases, dancefloors, in hotel cloakrooms, but so uncomfortable in our predicament that instead of greeting we pass one other in silence. It seems more considerate. Season mercifully over, two spoilt and bored young women with good but untilled minds, bumming around the smart spots of the capital and countryside, trying to find some excuse for being so vibrantly alive, and regularly failing. Is there nothing useful we can do that does not put either us or our parents to shame? Apparently not. Now and again we make stabs: look for jobs in the paper, pester our friends for suggestions, go for interviews, but our hearts are not in the search. I take a secretarial course and prove (it is my only apprenticeship failure in a lifetime) untrainable in this sphere. Eliza goes to work for one of her cousins who is opening a luxury restaurant somewhere in the city, but she never gets paid, and leaves. Then she walks dogs and loses one. Later, in desperation, she gets briefly engaged to another cousin, a different one from the tight-fisted restaurateur, and fills in a

sizeable amount of time unwrapping wedding presents and then wrapping them up again and sending them back.

5. Post Leander, post Michael, post engagement, and, so we have decided, post our earlier selves altogether. We are in the by now grey and battered Dauphine, Eliza and I alone, toiling and spluttering up the shadowy side of an Alpine pass on our way to Italy. Siena, we think. Perhaps San Gimignano. Somewhere small and friendly anyway, where we can get on with the challenging if slightly shameful task we have set ourselves: which, after all our posings as *femmes savantes* and *fatales* and what have you, is simply to buckle down and work for those wretched A levels we never got. Three each, the bare minimum that will then enable us to get into some university afterwards, even if it is only as external students, and study our new-found passion, philosophy. It is a tame enough target compared to some we have set ourselves, but in a way it's the most scary of all, for what if we fail?

5.1. 'We won't ruddy fail, you pusillanimous nit.' Again it is Eliza who has acted as spearhead. She has chosen the subjects, made the entries, squared our parents, even put us down on the register of some English school or other in Rome, where, in five months' time according to the courteous but somewhat fazed letter we have received from the principal, we are to sit for our exams. I have procured the syllabuses – syllabi? God, how will I ever pass Eng. Lit.? – and bought the books.

They are here with us, on the back seat of the car. By silent agreement we leave them there during our overnight stops, but so far they have not been stolen and now, with only one more night to go, still in the law-abiding north, it doesn't look as if they will be.

5.1.1. The poor Dauphine is really feeling the climb. I am animistic about cars and Eliza needs to pee, so we draw in at a filling station, manned by a leering, beetle-browed troll about seven-foot tall, and empty Eliza and fill the car, and then set off again. Or try to, because the car will not start.

5.1.2. At first we are unperturbed. The troll will right it, that after all is his job. But after we have watched him peer goofily into the engine for about four minutes on end without saying or doing anything except tap a heavy spanner against the palm of his hand and slaver, we begin to worry. Slightly. We look around for another source of help, but the station is deserted: it has grown suddenly dark and there is very little traffic on the road. We flank the troll on either side of the engine and begin questioning him: What is wrong? What can be done to right it? He lets out a snigger and leans backwards, surveying the hem of Eliza's miniskirt. '*Cassé*,' he says. 'Kaput.' And goes on with his palm-tapping. A few minutes later, from a kind of hut arrangement behind the petrol pumps, another troll appears and joins him – a slightly smaller exemplar but still huge. They snigger together over the dead engine and mumble words Eliza and I cannot grasp, and then, slowly and not in the least bit reassuringly, they spread out their arms and begin edging us, as if we were a couple of loose chickens to be rounded up, towards the hut.

5.1.3. It is an eerie moment: the solitude, the high, dark mountains, the sense of a danger that may still be imaginary, but at any moment may turn out to be real, especially once it is acknowledged. I don't need to say anything to Eliza, no hints, no warnings. I am confident as never before that everything that is going through my mind is going through hers, just as thoroughly and that much quicker. With faultless teamwork we make our progress – regress – as slow as possible, short of putting up resistance. In calm, unconcerned voices we speak of telephones, hotels, Michelin guide books, anything to keep the flame of normality alive.

5.1.4. This as far as the threshold. The inside of the hut, from what we can see of it as we approach, is designed to snuff the flame pretty quickly. There is a cooking stove inside and a mattress, laid flat on the floor, and worse still, there is a fat old woman bent over the stove, almost as tall as the trolls and very similar to look at, who gives one glance at Eliza and me and then shrugs her shoulders and lumbers out of the door in silence and makes off into the dusk.

5.1.5. It is at this point, when flight is our only hope and we have begun to exchange glances, expressing just this, that we hear the roar of several powerful and very much alive engines and the skidding of wheels, and a convoy of motor bikes swerves into the filling station and pulls to a halt in front of the pumps. It turns out to be a group of mathematicians – American – travelling south to a congress. In a trice the situation rights itself, or rather stays righted, it has never really quite gone wrong: Eliza and I introduce ourselves to the Americans, explain what has happened to the car, ask for a lift. We start to say something about the trolls as well but they are now being so helpful and ordinary it seems ridiculous, almost mean. One of the mathematicians puts his head into the entrails of the Dauphine and raises it again, an amused–cum–bemused expression on his face, and says to try starting the motor again now that he's reconnected the ignition. Should go, straight off. It does. We drive off under escort and dine with the mathematicians in Aosta. Delicious meal, delicious fizzy white wine to celebrate our rescue. On the way there Eliza and I dissect the experience, looking for conclusions to be drawn from it and arriving at just one: that Fate could never really have caught us, not in a trap like that, because WE ARE TOO BLOODY LUCKY.

6   For me, who seems at present the less favoured by fortune, if only minimally so, this boast holds good. But only for me. Eliza has a birthday in the spring and is given a sports car by her parents as a present. She says a decent car is the one thing we are lacking to make our lives perfect, and goes back to England to pick it up. On the way back, uncannily near the spot where we crossed with the trolls, the car, with yet another of her ubiquitous cousins at the wheel, crashes into a lorry carrying

fridges. The driver of the lorry is unhurt, so is the cousin, none of the fridges is in the least bit damaged, but Eliza is killed outright.

7. That is in May. One month later, right on schedule, I sit in a blisteringly hot Roman classroom among rows of noisy, sweaty candidates much younger than myself and hear Eliza's name read out by the invigilator. It is read at every session. The school knows she won't be sitting and knows why, but her name is on the roll-call and must therefore be read. Regulations. If it weren't so fascist I would like to stand up each time and shout out, 'Present,' because that is what she is to me: past, present and a handful of shards of future, rolled up into one beloved brown body I shall never see again.

8. I will hear her voice, however, often, and on this occasion it says, 'Sod that, you soppy nit, and get on with your paper.' So I do.

ROMA

An ageing beauty, huge, blowsy, lackadaisical, unkempt, totally indifferent to my feelings about her as indeed to those of her other countless admirers – not a likely candidate, you may think, for my next enduring passion, but such she was. Her name was Rome, and it was Eliza who brought us together with her choice of exam centre, and then left us together, to make of each other what we would.

The city's hold over me lasts to this day and I'm still hard put to say what it is based on. In those early days, when, exams taken and no good reason for remaining, I lingered on and on, deaf to my parents' pleas to return to England, I would probably have said the climate, the splendour of the site and buildings, the easy life, the easygoing natures of the inhabitants, the delicious food, the rapid access to the sea, countryside, mountains, lakes, or wherever you felt like going; more or less in this order. And probably, as a newcomer, I would have believed these reasons to be valid, and perceived them to be valid also.

And perhaps to some extent they were. Some of them. And still are, even though rapid access to anywhere, in *or* out of the city, is now but a memory inside greying heads, and splendour has to be glimpsed through the cracks that divide the tourist buses, clustered nose to tail around the perimeters of all the major sights. Certainly I slipped in easily enough myself. I found a flat, complete with flatmates, just by consulting the noticeboard of the school where I sat for the exams, and then making a telephone call. I found a job, quite a good one, running the office of a documentary-film director, simply by buying an English-language newspaper and making another call. A third call, to a number I had brought with me from home, and I held in my hand the first two cross-threads of a whole network of friends. (Mostly male, true, and mostly sex-obsessed, as Leander had forecast, but schooled to disappointment and therefore very easily deflected if need be. Not that it always was.) Within days I felt more secure and ensconced and at home than ever I had done in London. Or anywhere else for that matter.

I thanked the city, but had I paused to reflect I would have noticed that all the benefits so far had come, not from the heart of Rome itself, but from little foreign encrustations on its ventricles. The heart, when you got to know it, remained untouched, indifferent, beat to its own rhythm, pumped to its own requirements. Guests wanted to stay? *Affar' loro.* Their look-out. Space wasn't lacking: sixty more, a hundred more, five hundred more, what difference did it make? As long as they paid their way and didn't make unreasonable demands on the system. Like insisting that their papers be in order: foreigners were so obtuse about such things: nobody's papers should be in complete order as it left no room for helpful officials to perform favours, and favours and counter-favours were what the system was all about.

The climate, so renowned in the ancient world, was either a travellers' myth or else must have changed in the admittedly longish interval. I spent that first summer –

before I learnt to flee to the coast like everyone else –
in a darkened flat, with a bathtub filled with lukewarm
water into which I plunged myself at regular half-hour
intervals, else I think my blood would have turned to
gravy. Popular myth again had it that there was a marvellous
refreshing breeze called the Ponentino that got up at five
every afternoon, but I never knew it to blow in our
neighbourhood or indeed in any of the districts I ever
visited. The *portiere* of our apartment, a fierce critic of
local government, said it was on account of all the new
buildings that had gone up on the outskirts, blocking the
Ponentino's path.

Winters on the other hand were cruel, Nordic in character, without any of the North's domestic comforts to offset
them. It either rained sticky drizzle for a month on end,
or else a dry, barbed wind, undeterred by any amount of
building enterprise, chased through the streets, penetrating
clothing, rasping the skin, and teasing any hairstyle into a
stiff, backward-sweeping crest, reminiscent of the quills of
a porcupine under threat. Even my steel-wool kinks came
close to being straightened in the blast. The flat had three
beds in it, one double, and three threadbare Red Cross
blankets stored away in a cupboard. We slept under these
with coats and towels piled on top.

Spring, when it came, was all it was cracked up to be
and more but you could hardly admire it, so sleepy did
you get. April brought us a new flatmate, billeted on us
by a friend in the Food and Agriculture Organization of
the United Nations. She came preceded by a reputation
for martinet efficiency; we were told – worse, alerted –
that she was being especially shipped out from London by
the Organization to 'wield a new broom' in the Personnel
Department. We quaked and pushed a rather old broom

round the flat on our own account, trying to eliminate some of the fluff and pizza crumbs before she arrived, but we needn't have bothered. Rome neutralized her, defused her practically overnight. She got in from the airport, went straight to bed and slept for two and a half days before even telephoning her office. After that she rallied, but the blow to her pride was telling and she accepted the chaos of the flat with proportional meekness for the duration of her stay. Of our spare boarders, who came and went like viruses, staying for anything from a week to a month while they looked around for a more comfortable host, she was in fact the least troublesome we ever had. I no longer remember her name or anything much about her but I remember that we called her Honestly, because that was virtually all we ever heard her say. 'Honestly, look at me. Honestly, I don't know what's come over me. Honestly, honestly, how do you lot cope?'

Easy life – what about that one? *Could* it have been? I look around me now, hemmed in on all sides by what has surely become one of the most complicated living places in the world, and wonder. Looks helped, of course, youth helped, connections helped, being solvent helped, being foreign helped, and on these accounts other people helped too, with almost anything that needed doing, from opening a bank account to changing a tyre to cancelling a parking fine, so that life *felt* easy while you were actually living it, but was it really? Even for us?

Let me make a quick calculation. Three-quarters of an hour, regular waiting time for a bus. Half a morning: regular length of time spent queuing for any public service, whether it were posting a parcel or paying a gas bill or renewing your *permesso di soggiorno* or simply seeking information as to how any of these should be done. No, sorry, not queuing,

Romans don't queue: stampeding. Two seconds: the time it took, once you had reached the head of the stampede, to find out it was the wrong one and start all over again. Three months: the time it took to get our telephone connected, before we were given the magic name of Dr Rollo. (After which it took half a morning. But since it took a further couple of months to shake off Dr Rollo and his dodgy dinner invitations, in the end the advantage was not very great.) Nine daylight hours, the length of my wait in a grimy public-hospital corridor while Pilar, one of the more bothersome viruses, was having her wrists sewn up, which she had slit in a messy but superficial fashion in order to punish a faithless boyfriend. Nine gruelling lamplit hours with the bulb shining straight into my face: the length of my cross-examination afterwards in a police station. Did I know that it was a crime according to Italian law to drive a person to suicide? Did I know that it was also a crime to withhold information that could lead to the capture of a criminal guilty of such a crime, and that if I didn't talk I would end up in jail? What had led this young friend of mine, apparently so *ben sistemata*, to such a desperate step? *Who* had led her? Who had *pushed* her? Was there a man involved? No? Impossible, in these cases there was always a man involved. A cruel, cowardly, irresponsible *mascalzone* of a man. Think again, *Signorina*, and think carefully. What was his name? What did he look like? Where did he live?

I think this stubborn, malign, narrow-minded, vindictive policeman, so intent on unearthing evil where there was only foolishness, was probably the most unpleasant Roman I have ever met. But only probably and in no way exceptionally. Because the last putative virtue of the city, that of the easygoing nature of its inhabitants, is the biggest myth of all. Romans are not easygoing and the *vita* that they live is not *dolce*, anything but. They work long hard hours, and when they have what appears to be a cushy job like sitting on a chair in a museum telling you not to touch things, you can be sure they have another one, late into the night, which doesn't involve sitting at all. Whether metaphorically or in their brand-new cars, hooting and insulting one another as they go, they drive themselves extremely hard.

And as a result, or maybe it is a cause, they are among the worst-tempered people on the planet, and since they are literal-minded and bad about concealing things they are among the worst mannered also. The older generation foremost: I don't think I have ever come across so many rude over-seventies as I have in Rome; it is quite shocking. Such irritability, however, is vented in the private sphere and the private sphere only. Try standing in a crowded bank or post office or even a badly run supermarket and you will notice in the customers, far from rudeness, a docile resignation bordering on the angelic. Try to kindle them, and any sparks you get will bounce off against you instead. For being *difficile*, for refusing to *pazientare*, for causing a *disturbo*. In short, for exposing them to possible retaliation from anyone wearing anything resembling a uniform, be it only a till girl's stripy overall.

And retaliation will be forthcoming and furious, because, *non serviam*, the self-respecting Roman does not serve. He or she will accept a salary in return for sitting behind a glass partition or desk or counter and shoving things – forms, goods, stamps, pensions – in a surly fashion at the supplicant on the other side, but any attempt to define this activity as service will be quashed at source. By both parties, what is more, and for reasons of tact. Service is a dirty word; perhaps, in a covert fashion, one of the dirtiest in the entire dialect. Together with *fame*, hunger (to tell someone they are starving is in fact still, in these days of patent plenty, the most riling insult of all), *pezzente* which has its origin in the dignified Latin verb to petition or make a humble request, and *beccamorto*, or burier of the dead.

Willingness to serve, poverty, humility, the performance of works of mercy – Rome may have been for many centuries the centre of Christendom but the Sermon on the Mount never cut much ice with the native population, not if language is anything to go by. Uncharitable also by New Testament standards (and yet so widely used that they ring out more frequently than the bells, particularly in the fourfold rush hour), terms of abuse culled from illnesses such as tuberculosis and polio, or from simple shafts of misfortune: *A' tisico! A' paralitico! A' disgraziato!* No, Romans save up their admiration for other qualities: luck, success, cunning, caution, display of riches, veneer of erudition, personal tidiness, personal cleanliness, and a strict observance of even the most minute conventions, like never mixing blue handbags and black shoes, and keeping your smartest nightwear for when you are in hospital.

Where amongst all this ungrateful criticism is the voice of the lover of thirty years' standing? And where the grounds for my love? As I said at the outset, I find it difficult to say. All I can put forward in afterthought is the hypothesis, shaky and all too often shaken, that on the rare occasions when Rome lives up to her myths and offers you a really fine sight or a really fine day or a really fine meal or a really fine person, the quality of the gift is such that you are smitten *ex novo*, and willingly sign on for another thirty years of urban nightmare. Riven, as you know they will be, by shafts of dreamlike perfection unfindable in any other spot of the globe.

THE PROFESSOR

Eliza had led me to my favourite subject, and then, as a parting gift, to my favourite place on earth, but unfortunately the two didn't go very well together. Rome had a university all right and the university had a faculty of philosophy, and the faculty had a very liberal policy on admission so that my three scraped A levels more than entitled me to a place there, but the trouble was, the philosophy on offer just wasn't philosophy as I had learnt to recognize it. Eliza and I had swotted dutifully through our logic primers, drawing circles to represent classes and putting crosses in them to represent members, learning how to use reversed 'E's and sideways 'U's and triple dashes, and asking one another questions we hadn't asked since the nursery, such as, How do we know things? and, *Do* we really know things? and, Why should people be good? and, Could anyone invent a totally new colour? The Roman professor who interviewed me reacted to this approach, much as I seem to remember our nannies did, with impatience bordering on scorn, and fired other questions at me, concerning the One, the Absolute, the Phenomenon, the Thing in Itself. When he saw my notebooks with the squiggles and the rings and the shaded segments, he suggested with a trace of alarm I had perhaps come to the wrong faculty. Could I have been looking for Architecture? It was in quite another part of the city. We left one another shortly afterwards with a reciprocal feeling of lucky escape.

And so it was that I enrolled in a correspondence college instead. The best of both worlds, or at any rate both countries: the warm Italian sun on my body, cool shafts of English common sense into my mind. The institute I chose was called Fitzroy Hall. It sent me pictures of itself while I was making up my mind, presumably to convince me of its solidity, perhaps of its very existence, but they were engravings, not photographs, executed against a blank background with a curlicue motto on the front where the door should be, and if anything contravened their purpose. Nor was I much reassured by a description, on the opposite page, of the college tie, which the brochure told me could be mine on enrolment for the sum of £4 16/6d, plus postage.

However, if not in bricks at least in function, the college existed all right and lost little time proving it. Only sixteen days after I posted off my cheque and entry form (nanoseconds by the standards of the Italian post), batches of bulky envelopes started to pelt through the mail at me, containing reams and reams of printed information on every branch, twig, leaf and vein of philosophy I could have wished for (and often more). These were my lesson sheets. They came in envelopes of different colours – one for each sub-subject: green for logic, pink for ethics, mauve for metaphysics, and so forth – and would continue to do so, at the rhythm of one a week, for the duration of the entire course. Each one needed reading, studying, mulling over, possibly with the aid of further reading matter, and then answering. In essay form. Anything from two pages upwards.

And this was only, as it were, the grape shot, the first light sprinkle of the Fitzroy Hall artillery; the cannon balls proper, in the form of books, most of them of truly leaden weight, were still to arrive.

For the first few months or so, until I starched myself with discipline and devised a proper timetable for study, I floundered unhappily among this growing mass of multi-coloured knowledge to be absorbed, and dreaded the arrival of each new packet – the mauve ones in particular, which stood not only for metaphysics but mist and muddle too: even after the third instalment I scarcely knew what was meant by the term.

Thankfully, though, provided its students fulfilled their part of the bargain (which in terms of effort I would put at around 89 per cent), the Fitzroy system was every bit as good as the brochure promised. And gradually, as the weeks wore on and my familiarity with the subject increased, I stopped dreading the flux of brightly coloured envelopes and began on the contrary to look forward to it. Although what I really looked forward to most were the white envelopes – the ones that contained my own essays, winging back to me after a brief roost on the brickless masonry of Fitzroy Hall, bearing comments from a faceless, nameless tutor.

I say comments because I expected comments and longed for comments. Solo study is a very lonely business, and I missed Eliza more than I would have done my left-hand middle finger or several dioptres. But what in fact the scheme provided was simply the correction of the most glaring spelling mistakes, a scribbled signature on the part of the corrector at the start and end of the essay to show it had been read all through, and a mark in the range of Poor to Excellent.

For a while, at least another three or four months, I thrived well on this meagre diet. A Good and I was happy for days, a Very Good, of which I got one, in bright-green ink, for Bacon, set up a wave of glee on which I crested for almost a fortnight. But deeper down the intellectual loneliness continued. My English flatmates resented my absorption and the fact that I did even less housework than before, if this were possible; my Italian friends just thought I was a trifle mad. *Filosofia*? You did that at school. At university, if you were clever you did physics or engineering, and if you were dim you did languages or political science. Nobody did *Filosofia*. *Non si usa*. It was not the custom.

By the time the sixth month came my life had become so schizoid, and I along with it, that I think I might shortly have abandoned study altogether as incompatible with social life, full stop. But then something happened that made me take heart. An essay came back with a personal touch to it, such as neither tutor nor pupil was supposed to add, not according to the regulations. I could hardly believe my eyes. 'Very acute thinking here,' was written in the margin in a spiky Gothic hand. 'You show a real talent. Congratulations. Could you tell me a little more about yourself, I wonder, at the foot of your next essay?'

Nothing, an extended fingertip, but to me it was as if I had been clasped to the hairy Greek bosom of Socrates himself. The 'little' was difficult to keep to, but at the end of my next essay I duly penned a word portrait of myself: age, background, education to date, and one or two lines about what I was doing in Rome and why I had opted for this particular course. I longed to add more but was frightened, once I raised the floodgates on my enthusiasm, of sweeping the recipient away in the torrent.

I needn't have worried. Professor Logan, as he identified himself by return of post, turned out to be as keen a correspondent as I was myself. The next white envelope brought back my essay, generously marked, and a long footnote to my footnote, full of elegant touches like 'viz' and 'though' spelt 'tho' and '*Pace*' to express disagreement, saying how thankless the task of postal tutor normally was and how delightful and refreshing it was '*per contra*' to meet with someone who appeared not only to endure but actually benefit from his tuition. After that, we left off essay bottoms as being too restricting and passed to letters proper, on separate sheets of paper. In all, at the rate of one a week each, we must have exchanged something like three hundred letters before the course was up.

I kept no copies and only a handful or so of the originals – as curios. I wonder what we said? As far as I can see from the ones I did keep, on my side it was mostly sweeping speculation very carelessly worked out, and on my tutor's, a constant, patient attempt to get me to do just the opposite: drop my broom and start using a toothcomb instead. 'Attention. In logic there are no degrees of truth', I see he has written at one point, presumably in regard to something I had described as very true, or quite true, or fairly true. 'An assertion is either true or false, and there's an end on it.' And I seem to remember scribbling off a reply, indignant, excited, my brain-cogs smoking with friction: 'Why no degrees of truth in logic, for goodness sake? Why do we have to kowtow to digital laws when we aren't computers? Why can't we adopt a system with a sliding scale of values, like in probability theory?' Oh, I was an eager student all right, full of what I regularly thought were unprecedented insights into all the standard problems, but which just as regularly turned out to be as hoary and chewed-over as the problems themselves. 'What was Descartes thinking of when he chose his famous Cogito as cornerstone? Didn't he realize that it was only as a *social* animal that man could achieve consciousness of self?' (No, but Nietzsche did. In 1882. Bother.) 'Conflict in Machiavelli can be resolved, surely, if we read *The Prince* as an extended satire throughout?' (A hard view to maintain, and anyway Alfieri put it forward four hundred years ago, for what it was worth. Bother again. Bother, bother, bother.) Take a bite at Marx's theory of value then, must be something as yet unmasticated to get my teeth into there.

Professor Logan guided me throughout all these sallies on a long, slack leash, never interfering with my progress, no matter how wrong-headed, but never abandoning me either. More and more I came to count on his invisible presence, more and more I came to relish the sight of his gargoyley 's's and ogival 'o's. Of which, I may add, there were happily more and more to see: over the months his letters grew steadily longer and friendlier, sometimes containing truly exhilarating passages like, 'May I call you Zoë now that I have, as it were, seen your mind without its *stola* on?' (Help, what was a *stola*?) 'Please for your part call me Giles.' 'Sorry to hear you have had trouble with your wisdom teeth. May their cutting presage the growth of wisdom *per se*!'

After two years we had become so intimate as to exchange photographs. I can't remember which of us suggested it; perhaps, out of a kind of Hegelian necessity, one step, two step and do the Hokey Cokey, it just happened. 'Delightful,' Professor Logan commented on mine (I had difficulty still in thinking of him as Giles.) 'Delightful to learn that the image of you which thus far I have borne in my head, agreeable tho' it was, is far outshone by reality. On a par with Plato's prisoners confronted by the sun (*vide* Republic, book 7), I step out of my cave and am blinded.'

My tribute, I am afraid, was less fulsome, on account of the Professor – Giles – being shown up by the camera as a man of fifty or more years, with protruding eyes that looked as if they were just kept in their sockets by glasses, and a shiny, narrow, tortoisey head, imperfectly covered by a long slick of hair stemming from somewhere close above the ear. But then, what did it matter? Socrates was ugly. I had a hunch Leibniz was too. Rousseau with his catheter and nightcap in place couldn't have been much to look at either. Schopenhauer had clearly no sex appeal at all. Kant ditto. In fact the more I thought about it the harder pressed I was to think of one single philosopher famed for looks, with the possible exception of Bertrand Russell, *many* years and wrinkles back.

'Thank you very much for the photograph,' I wrote. 'From the sunshine it looks as if it was taken in Greece, only of course you wouldn't have had your dog with you there. I love rough-haired dachshunds, they are my absolute favourites.' (This was to earn me another reprimand: there are no degrees of favouritism either.) 'Yours looks a poppet. I have put it on my desk' (this second error, far graver to my mind, was passed without comment) 'since it is, as you say, much nicer to write to someone with a real face instead of addressing yourself to a blank.'

And I think it was. After a short running-in period during which I focused for preference on the dachshund, I became used to my mentor's likeness and began to find it – not attractive exactly, that would be going too far, but comforting, companionable, at times even inspiring. In a philosophical way. The eyes behind the lenses looked so wonderfully wise; the short-sleeved terylene shirt and heavy sandals vouched for such a pure, unworldly character in their wearer. And these, in an intellectual friendship such as ours, were surely the only qualities that counted: power of intellect and loftiness of stance *vis-à-vis* the trivia. (Note my prose, how polished it was becoming under his sway.) Nothing else.

It's probably lucky that our actual physical meeting didn't take place until after I had sat for my finals and passed them: with my philosophess's pride taking the knocking it did, I don't know I'd have been able to write a line. But let me tell things in order.

When the results came in Professor Logan wrote to congratulate me and suggested, to my immeasurable gratification, I continue my studies at post-graduate level. 'We could meet when next you are in London,' his letter ended, 'to discuss the matter. Over a luncheon if you are willing. I know of a very pleasant little Greek restaurant that will be admirably in keeping.' And he added a telephone number, requesting me to get in touch on my arrival.

How could I not be willing? I was straining at the leash (no longer slack under all the tugging), I was tripping over myself. My first bona fide Mind Admirer. The first man ever to be attracted to me by mental means alone, without the auxiliary aid of so much as a smile or a glance or a voice tone. Why, for two whole years the poor man hadn't even known what I looked like. How could I fail to want to meet such a person, representing as he did my hardest-won and proudest conquest to date?

In my impatience I didn't reply to the invitation in

writing this time but picked up the telephone instead and dialled the number I'd been given. A woman's voice answered, civil but guarded. His wife? Must be a fascinating person too. She listened while I poured out what amounted in the telling to a rather complicated explanation, and said (so briskly that I changed my mind and decided she must be a secretary, and a very efficient one at that) she would refer everything to Professor Logan at the earliest opportunity, thank you and goodbye.

Once in London I rang again, and this time I got a male voice. The Professor's. No, Giles's, GILES's. Now that I was about to meet him I must master that Christian name. The voice was higher than I expected and slightly irregular: if I hadn't known what a serious-minded person it belonged to I would have thought in patches it was giggling. It went a bit faint too when it got to the time and place of our appointment. (Which probably explained things: we had got a bad line.) It also had an accent Eliza would have imitated beautifully, but I tried not to notice this since there is no place for snobbery in the trained philosopher's mind.

And the meeting – well, details apart, you can probably imagine by now how it went off and what went wrong and why, but I still hadn't a clue of what lay in store. I was still thinking in terms of *thinking*, more fool I. Fancying myself as a Diotima, supping with Socrates, flambéing his food with the sparks of my brilliance, wowing him flat. (I wonder incidentally if that lady ever had to contend, during a symposium, with a problem of this kind? A goatskin or something in place of a handbag?) And fearful at the same time of just the opposite: of being a dud, a disappointment, with my live conversation falling miserably below the level which I was confident I had attained in my letters.

Both unnecessary – fears *and* fancies. I entered the restaurant, picked out the Professor immediately and was just about to cross over to his table and say an awestruck hello, when a woman of whom I registered little save that she had a tight perm and was wearing a red suit, also tight, rushed over to me and without any warning swung a heavy leather handbag right into my face. It hit me like a punchball and I swung backwards on my own account, colliding with another customer who had entered the restaurant behind me. He in turn, or perhaps it was a she, I can't say I had the leisure to notice which, ricocheted sideways, jolting into an occupied table and upsetting everything it held. It was not a dignified entry for an aspiring Ph.D.

After the crash there was silence, not a long one but long enough for the woman to say to me, and be heard saying it by pretty well everyone present, 'Keep away from him, you scheming little slut. You thought you'd got him, didn't you, but you're wrong, he's mine and don't you forget it.' After which outburst she strode from the restaurant on her tight-encased, muscular thighs, swinging the punchball as she went.

I'm not sure what I did or said in reply. Being as always slow on the uptake I think I just said OK, rather feebly, to the woman's departing figure, and then, even more feebly, began to offer scattered apologies – to the waiters, the other diners, and then to the Professor himself, who had left his table and was now standing beside me, holding out a limp and slightly shaky hand.

I thought things might be saveable – just for an instant, before I saw the cause of the shakes. Then I realized (and it was as if I had been bag-lobbed again on the other cheek, a good sight harder) that the man was giggling uncontrollably. He had been giggling on the telephone, already helpless to check himself, and he was giggling now. With vanity, delight, or a foretaste of sexual excitement, it mattered little which and I didn't care to investigate, but he was clearly giggling himself silly.

'Come and sit down, Zoë,' he spluttered through the giggles. He pronounced my name Zooey and now I allowed myself, in paltry revenge, to mark this against him. 'We'll have a little talk and straighten things out, right? How about starting with some vine leaves, eh, I'm told they're very tasty.'

Maybe, but to me they tasted of nothing. I swallowed one, more or less whole, disposed partially of a second by parking it under my tongue, and then begged to be excused and made blindly towards the bathroom. From there, without entering, I went into the kitchen and left by the back exit.

This was not the end of my student's career in philosophy for in fact I enrolled for my Ph.D. and went on studying, on and off, and then offer and offer, for quite a few years before I quitted, but it was the beginning of the end. Wittgenstein says somewhere that philosophy is a disease of the mind: if so, then the swipe I received was not a deathblow at all but a therapeutic thump that brought me to my senses, and I ought to be grateful to the energetic red-sheathed Xantippe. But for some reason it still riles me to probe, I am not.

THE LADY KILLER

To say I loved just a city and a discipline, although true for the time being, is to give a very misleading picture of my man-filled Roman life. Our men-filled Roman lives. My two abiding flatmates, Lola and Perdita (who had to change to being Paddy when it was discreetly pointed out to her that her name in Italian meant discharge), were both young and attractive, and uninhibited according to local standards, and our flat, long before I reached it, was already a Mecca for all sorts of secular pilgrims, mostly but not exclusively of male gender.

Some of them, but relatively few considering, were drawn there by personal motives: Paddy had a regular boyfriend she eventually married – years later, when divorce was introduced; Lola had two she had to juggle; occasionally one of the viruses would turn out to be a siren and bring along a whole captivated crew. For another group, slightly more numerous, the lure was the wider one of our nationality. (Although it is hard to retrace today the enormous masculine prestige there was in being seen around with a Northern-European female anywhere between the sixty mark and twelve; it seems a piece of Latin history as remote as the Punic wars.) The majority however simply came, like skiers to the mountains, for the air and the outing and the sense of freedom that the flat itself, more than our company, seemed to provide. Asking little more than to be allowed to sprawl there quietly in a corner, mouthing English phrases, playing our records, leafing through our magazines, thirstily absorbing what they took to be the latest oscillations of our staid old capital in its swinging stage.

Or else just sprawling, happy to be there, in a state of borrowed and temporary independence from *La Famiglia*. One, name of Federico, so stable you could have used him as a lampstand, we eventually got tired of and banished, but had to relent again when he told us that at home he shared a bedroom with his ninety-year-old grandmother. Not for space reasons – the family home was large – but because the old lady was frightened of the dark. The arrangement had started with his grandfather's death when Federico was ten, and now, twenty-three years on, there was no changing it: abandoned to the *tenebrae*, Nonna might die of fright, and what would Federico's mother say then?

Sometimes it was nice to have all these generic admirers filling in the scene, sometimes less so, sometimes downright annoying. We had a Sardinian journalist, for example, who fell in love with all three of us in turn, mercilessly unrequited, and spent twenty-two nights – roughly a week for each brief passion – curled on a pile of spare bath mats on the floor, moaning his love into the nap. When we evicted him and shut not only the flat door on him but the downstairs door and the gate outside, he shamed us into readmittance by ringing the bells of all the other flats and broadcasting his love over the newly installed intercom. This was a terrible *disturbo* and very *sconveniente* and, just what you would expect when you let a *signorile* flat to a set of fast foreign hussies like ourselves. Deeper

in the mire than we slipped our landlord and landlady,
and up, in consequence, went the monthly rent by a full
three thousand lire.

Less flamboyant but still more annoying, in that there
was no flattery to temper the disturbance, were what we
called the Kashmiris, cashmere being the uniform that all
of them wore, whether jacket or overcoat or what they
again without exception called the 'pull'. These were a
group of thirty to forty year olds, mostly aristocrats, mostly
interconnected, mostly bearers of droll little nicknames like
Dado and Tinti and Bubi and Bibi behind which lurked
yards of real nomenclature, and mostly if not exclusively
on the look-out, in a rapacious, single-minded manner,
for a profitable blend of sex and English conversation for
which they were prepared to give absolutely nothing in
return. Neither time, nor friendship, nor even a smattering
of Italian nor the address of the shop (no, warehouse) where
they bought their magnificent winter woollies.

Usually we could tell them at a glance – or at a touch.
And usually we avoided them. Reminding one another,
if any of us was tempted to forget (and they *were* rather
alluring some of them, I must admit, in their Pucci-Gucci
way), of the long list of Anglophone victims strewing their
devious patrician paths. One afternoon, however, when I
was alone in the flat doing some typing work I had brought
home with me – my job was luckily of this nice pliable sort
– I received a visit from an archetypal representative of the
genre, who strangely I felt no inclination to avoid at all.
Not even after he had doffed his 'pull' to reveal a silk shirt
embossed with coroneted monogram, and flopped down
on the sofa beside me and lit a flattened Turkish cigarette
and inserted it into an appositely flattened ivory holder
and brushed a casual hand across the meeting place of my

thighs to remove ash he had dropped there by what he called mistake. *Peccato* to spoil my *chicchissimo* skirt. (This was a favourite ploy of all Kashmiris, incidentally: the masked advance: the wine stain on your shirtfront, the ill-fitting belt that needed tightening, the birdshit you just might have sat on in the open-air restaurant, but let them check, let them check. And since they were all so fanatically clothes-conscious you could never be sure the concern wasn't genuine and you just fancying you were being fancied. Which then compounded your flurry, leaving you feeling tatty and shat-on and conceited all at once.)

By the time Lola and Paddy got back I had already conversed with this particular specimen for three solid hours (quite a record, for the Kashmiris were laconic as a rule), covering topics as diverse as Napoleon and spiritism and nursery puddings, been for a farewell drink with him in the bar round the corner – still chattering my nut off, he was proving so receptive – and accepted an invitation to a large and impressive-sounding dinner party he was giving in his nearby Parioli apartment that very evening.

My more seasoned friends were disgusted by my naïveté and lack of discernment, and so incredulous to begin with as to think I must be teasing. A dinner date? With one of those smarmy charmies? At first sighting? Alone? On enemy ground? Come off it, surely I wasn't serious? Because I knew what I'd be in for, didn't I, if I went? A *garçonnière*, and a table laid for two, and grub on it if I was lucky but probably not, just a half-bottle of inferior fizzy white wine, and then a beeline for the bedroom and a couple of grunts and a shudder and *Grazie tanto*, and back in a taxi that I'd have to pay for myself. How did the blighter get wind of us anyway? Who told him about us? Who gave him our address?

I thought I could detect here, mingled with their concern, just a tiny strand of envy. We never admitted as much, but our vaccination against the Kashmiri set had never really taken properly. At least mine hadn't. We scorned them as philanderers, and rightly, but lurking behind the scorn there was always that niggling element of sour grapes, of dissatisfaction at a challenge funked. '*Vedrai che tu sei quella . . .*' sings Don Giovanni to Elvira, conning her for the umpteenth time: there have been hundreds of women before and after, but she is the only one he really loves. The chances of this being true are close to zero, as poor Elvira soon discovers, tripping down in her nightie into the arms of a sniggering Leporello. But oh, what a boost to the morale if the gamble comes off; if the roles of hunter and quarry are reversed and the arch-seducer is himself seduced. By you. The arch-seductress. The one and only.

'I'm not sure who sent him,' I had to admit, because in my heightened state I hadn't dwelt on his credentials. 'I think it must have been Lorenzo. He knows Lorenzo anyway, he said they play cards together sometimes and used to go to the same school.'

'Ah, Lorenzo.' That made a slight difference. Lorenzo was a trusty, almost as solid a fixture in our lives as Federico was. Kind, unmarried, capon-like, possibly kinky and thus recompensed by the huge amount of grubby underwear to be found there, he would call by at the flat almost every evening, after the closing of his office, and keep us company while we dressed to go out. All our problems passed first, as a matter of course, into his pudgy capable hands, and I would say about 90 per cent never went any further. He was lawyer to us – this in fact was his profession – but also plumber, electrician, tourist guide, beauty consultant, social secretary, bath-runner and, to the extent it was permitted him, shepherd as well.

Paddy's finger was already inserted in the telephone dial, forming Lorenzo's number. 'Whass this pretty boy's name?' she growled. 'I'm gonna check on him, just to make sure.'

The pretty boy's name was arguably one of the prettiest things about him (despite its English rendering being roughly Elvis Myrtle Greenhouse), so I gave it with a certain flourish. 'Alvise Mirto di Villaverde.'

'Good,' said Paddy, stubbornly practical. 'Then there are unlikely to be two of them.'

Lorenzo was not in his office to be consulted, but he turned up anyway ten minutes or so later, just as I was preparing to leave. His reaction was decidedly negative, even taking into account his rumbling jealousy of all our male acquaintances. 'Alvise Mirto? Oh my God, Zoettina, I wouldn't if I were you. The fellow is a . . .' He paused while he searched for a suitable word in his large if a trifle old-fashioned English vocabulary. I expected shit, rotter, perhaps even scoundrel or bounder, but no, button was the rather intriguing verdict he came up with.

'*Button*?' Long-winded people are sometimes said in Italian to sew buttons on their listeners; this was the only connection I could see. 'You mean he's boring, Lawrence? He didn't seem boring to me. Quite the opposite.'

Lorenzo looked deeply offended, as he always did if any of his carefully rehearsed idioms misfired. 'Not button, *stupidina*, *budden*. He's a budden, a real budden.'

Lola was the first to catch his meaning, and went, 'Cor!' before she could stop herself. I could tell she felt the same way I did about the challenge. 'A bad'un! Then it wasn't you who sent him round to us, naughty Lawrence, was it?'

Lorenzo pursed his already tiny mouth to show still deeper offence. '*Mia cara ragazza*, what do you take me for? *Un ruffiano*? A ruffian?'

Tactfully Lola let ruffian pass for whatever was intended. Probably pimp. 'But you know him?' she insisted. 'You play cards with him? You went to the same school?'

He shrugged. 'I have played cards with him a few times, yes. Poker. But never again. And we went to the same school for about a fortnight, before he was expelled.'

More and more intriguing. 'You mean he cheats?'

Lorenzo shook his head; fairness was part of his code. 'No,' he said, 'not cheats exactly, but he plays a hard mean game. Between friends, you know, there is a sort of agreement not to raise the stakes beyond a certain point . . . Well, he doesn't stick by that, he knows what your limit is and he kind of jumps at you and pushes you over it, so you take fright and go away without seeing.'

Brought up in a card-playing household, this sounded to me like the very best Poker behaviour. And inadvertently Lorenzo had let slip that he and the beautiful bad'un were indeed friends – of a sort. I decided I would never forgive myself if I chickened out at this stage. First, though, I had better find out all I could.

'What was he expelled from school for?'

But sadly, or perhaps happily, Lorenzo couldn't remember. It might have been something to do with betting – organizing some phoney lottery or sweepstake and pocketing all the money. Or else it was girls. Definitely it was girls later on, when there was that nasty business of the rape charge . . .

'*Rape charge*?' All three of us this time. Oh dear, I wished he hadn't mentioned this, it made it more difficult for the Cavalier in me to triumph over the Roundhead.

Yes, well, Lorenzo admitted, perhaps he shouldn't have said that, because nothing was ever proved. In fact he didn't think things had ever got to the court stage. But they got into the papers all right. Headlines in the gossip mags: 'Sadistic *Marchese*', 'American Beauty Meets Italian Beast', stuff like that. Some people say the family spooned out and there was a cover-up, and others say the girl was to blame and only accused him out of spite because he dunked her, but anyway there was a great stink, and a great shadow cast over the *Marchese*'s character, and polite society refused to have any more to do with him. If I was foolhardy enough as to go to this dinner, all I would meet there would be film people and artists and disreputable rakes like Alvise Mirto himself.

This was intended to deter, as indeed was the whole portrait, but Lorenzo's many skills didn't include psychology, and the mad-bad-and-dangerous-to-know result was nigh irresistible. Film people, too, I longed to meet film people.

So you could delete the nigh. Five minutes later, having applied my thickest make-up and changed into my darkest and slinkiest dress so as not to appear the *ingénue* that I felt, I was out of the flat and on my way to this place of likely perdition, driving myself in my own car so that at least the prediction of the taxi ride would prove untrue. In my bag – last-minute concession to the fright my friends had managed to instil in me – a survival kit consisting of a scrap of paper bearing Lorenzo's home telephone number, two telephone counters (in case I had to make my SOS from a public phone), a rusty dog whistle that only worked if you blew into it from a certain angle, but never mind, need made a good goniometer, and – for use *in extremis*, only if the worst came to the very very worst – a huge long carving knife used for slicing *prosciutto*.

Not in the least reassured, in fact doubly scared by this improvised weaponry jingling at my side, I reached my dinner host's flat in a state of near panic. I say flat, as he did, but in fact the building was a house, an elegant, slightly sad-looking turn-of-the-century villa, set in a large overgrown garden. It seemed strangely quiet for the venue of a well-attended reception such as had been described to me, but Romans scorn punctuality as a provincial habit, so I reckoned I was simply, in my provincial way, the first to arrive.

I rang the doorbell, and after a longish wait the door was opened by a Filipino manservant who giggled at me in the penumbra and beckoned me to follow him up a flight of stairs. '*Marchese sopra*,' he said.

Sopra didn't sound quite right either for dining purposes, but the presence of a third person reassured me and I did as I was requested. Relaxing yet further when, having reached the top of the stairs, I was shown through a door and into a large prettily lit attic, furnished as a sitting-cum-dining room, definitely not as a bedroom.

However my relaxation was brief – five to ten seconds, not more – because once inside the room almost the first item of furniture my eyes rested on (or rather lit on and then bounced off horrified, not resting at all) was a dinner table laid for – yes, you've got it, for two. Not even for three for appearances' sake, but a brazen, uncompromising two. Empty of nourishment, just as Paddy had forecast. Not even a miserable salt cellar.

The Filipino took my coat with another giggle – politeness, I now imagine, but it didn't sound like that at the time – and asked me if I would like to leave my bag with him also.

My bag? Nobody was separating me from my bag. Not even my host himself, who now came smilingly across the parquet floor to meet me, a glass of straw-coloured liquid in his hand. The shifty toad. Fizzy white wine? No, it was champagne, but that was a mere technicality.

I shook my head in stern refusal. More difficult than it sounds, because fear was turning my neck all rigid. 'And the other guests?' I asked in a throttled voice. 'You said it was a dinner party. When are they coming?'

I thought I could see him pondering the alternatives of candid caddishness on the one hand and tortuous lying on the other. But I was evidently wrong, or else he simply fused the two to avoid the bother, because what he came out with were candid lies. So nonchalantly delivered as to constitute an extra offence in themselves.

'You won't believe it,' he said, 'but they all let me down. One after the other. So sorry, Alvise, but we cannot come. Very rude, no? I wanted to warn you and invite you for another evening, but this seemed rude too. On my part. When you had got all ready and dressed yourself' – he took a step forward and placed a finger on my shoulder strap – 'in this beautiful, seckasy dress . . .'

He was right, I couldn't believe it. I couldn't believe, one, that anyone could be so duplicitous as he was – chatting me up all afternoon on Austerlitz and apple crumble and then turning into this humourless circus werewolf. And, two, I couldn't believe that anyone could be quite so stupid as myself. I had been warned and rewarned, the trap had been described to me in minutest detail, and out of sheer, idiotic presumption (because, forget the talk of risk and courage, that was what it was), I had chosen to ignore both warnings and description and to walk slap into its unsprung jaws.

With no notion, moreover, of how to walk out of it again, or better still, run. It sounds feeble, and it was feeble, but even stronger than my fear was my embarrassment. Embarrassment at having to make the situation explicit. At having to admit that I had been taken in by him like the greenest, goofiest novice at the game. Above all embarrassment at having to make a scene, which I knew anyway, if he was the tough professional Lorenzo made him out to be (and it darn-well looked as if he was), he would manage to turn to his advantage. Call him a liar, and I would get more of those flat, insouciant, take-it-or-leave-it lies. Protest, and he might drop the fiction of the lies and get nasty. Scream, and he might get *really* nasty. Try to make a run for it, and I would most likely find myself tackled and felled. And once I was down . . . Oho, once I was down . . .

So I did nothing. Made no fuss, no bones, no trouble at all. I drank the champagne when it was pressed on me a second time, responded automatically to the equally automatic courtship, and when the Filipino came in with a napkin on his arm and asked if we were ready for dinner (so there was at least to be the garnish of food), I sat myself down, zombie-fashion, at the incriminating table and prepared for the ordeal of cramming a whole meal down my semi-paralysed throat, with no appetite whatever, with no apparent reluctance whatever.

'Perhaps you'd like to give that to Patricio?' my captor suggested in quite a kindly voice, indicating the bag, still firmly clamped under my fork-wielding arm. 'Before the *fettuccine* arrive, I mean?'

And it was then that the inspiration came, or the first

dawning of it. 'No thanks,' I said, still outwardly zombie, but gradually reviving inside as the idea consolidated and took shape. 'I . . . um . . . I never leave go of my bag nowadays, you see, not after the assault.'

'Assault?' For the first time that evening my host's voice contained a flicker of his earlier interest. Since my entry he had evidently counted me as just another trophy, eight-tenths won.

'Yes,' I said, translating all the key terms for the sake of impact. 'Assault. *Aggressione*.' And rapidly cobbled together some story of how I had been set on by a would-be rapist the year before when I was in London, and how I'd had to go into psychiatric care on account of the shock and upset to my nervous system.

His voice became more interested and more pensive as he repeated the terms, *psichiatra*, *trattamento*, *squilibrio nervoso*, several times half-aloud to himself in the wake of mine. 'And what has the . . . er . . . handbag to do with all this?' he asked, a trifle uncertainly, when I had finished.

'Nothing really,' I replied. 'It's just that, well, you know, if anyone should ever make another attempt, then . . . GRRRAH!' And so saying, or rather roaring, I whipped out the *prosciutto* knife and made with it what I hoped was a sufficiently *squilibrato* lunge in the air.

I hadn't had time to consider the consequences of this gesture, but if I had I don't think the one that actually ensued would ever have occurred to me. There was a silence and a gasp followed by a gentle little puff of exhaled breath, and then a thin, drawn-out squeaky noise as the rubber-soled shoes of the Marchese – his Clairck, as he would no doubt have called them – preceded their wearer's limp body in its downward slide from chair to floor. He had fainted clean away.

When the manservant rushed in, alerted by the noise of the falling chair, I was tempted to point to the table and say *Marchese sotto*, it seemed so symmetrical. But I didn't of course, I said *Marchese malato*, instead, in a genuinely worried voice, and left it at that.

On my way downstairs (minus overcoat, which came back later via Lorenzo, stuffed any old how into a contemptuous supermarket paper bag) I could hear the Filipino telephoning for the doctor, repeating this phrase into the mouthpiece – *Marchese malato, malatissimo* – and giggling his head off.

Once safely inside my car and engine started, I began, a titch unsteadily at first, to do the same.

MEETING

Now and then a bedroom farce, a comedy of manners, a drama – fortunately of teapot size – but the scenario of the flat was productive above all of romance, of a rather domesticated kind. This being so, I suppose it was inevitable sooner or later that one of our visitors, more enterprising than the rest or simply more tenacious, should edge himself into a position of habitual partner as far as I was concerned. It had happened to Paddy, it had happened – twice simultaneously – to Lola, and now, slowly but surely, without my greatly noticing, it began happening to me.

Paddy and Lola were critical of the development, and not entirely without reason. They called the man in question the frog. Not because he spoke French, which he did, being Belgian; not because of his prominent eyes or croaky laugh or ability to thrive in different elements, all of which he had too, to be scrupulously accurate; but because they insisted he was exactly that: a frog that I was willing into a prince by the triple means of kissing him, keeping my eyes tight shut thereafter, and wearing heavy metaphorical gardening gloves to prevent myself learning of the failed transformation. In short that I was kidding myself I was to any degree in love.

143

And they may have been right, but to me it seemed a logical enough step to take. (No, not logical, Professor Logan was already hard at work on my vocabulary and 'logical', slackly used, was one of his worst bugbears; let me say a compelling enough step.) And a compelling enough person too. My eyes may have been narrowed slightly but they definitely weren't shut, nor were the gloves so thick as to rob me of my powers of feeling. I was fond of Charles, I liked him, I liked being with him.

OK, he was pushy, and dead set on furthering his diplomatic career, and desperately vain and rather too highly strung for my liking, but he was also extremely intelligent and tender and ironic, and if not the first to make fun of himself then a close enough second. Added to which he was deeply sensual when it came to things like food and wine and sun and textures (and even soap and scent and flowers: I've never known anyone so alive to smells), and he amused me and comforted me no end and kept me very good company for the best – no, not the best but the most sizeable – part of a year. Sexually he was volatile and nomadic, which constituted indeed his main charm in my eyes, but he was trapped to fascination point by my rawness and total incapacity to climax in any hands other than my own, and made a very dedicated lover in his strange tense way. *Pace* Paddy and Lola, he was really something of a prize.

Our relationship might have lasted longer, become even closer, had it not been for the fact that one evening, when we were meant to be going out to dinner together prior to some dreary embassy function, he rang at the last moment to say that he had had a slight accident with his car and would have to skip dinner and go straight on to the reception. Would I join him there, or would I prefer to give the whole thing a miss?

I was never the right shape to fit comfortably into diplomatic circles. I chose the second alternative and went out with the faithful Federico instead, who took me to what turned out to be an even less congenial gathering where two rigid lines of po-faced young people – the girls in black, without exception, the men in tight grey *fumo di Londra* suits and stiff high collars that hardly permitted head movement – were practising with Italo-Prussian severity the steps of the Hully Gully. Federico slotted himself with no apparent reluctance into one of the lines and began his training. I, feeling old and sophisticated and regretting Charles and dinner and even, just for a moment, the embassy environment, wandered out on to the terrace where I came across a fellow deserter: a man, sitting alone in the far corner on a swing-chair, in a darkness so deep I couldn't see any of his features except the rims of his nostrils when he inhaled his cigarette, and the upper curve of his chin. Inexplicably, on the basis of the three faint parabolas, I felt strongly drawn towards him.

We spoke for a while, but not easily. He had the unfashionable attribute, which I love and used to share and regret terribly now that I have lost it, of being shy. I don't remember what we spoke about, but I remember that the first moment of authentic contact between us came when he asked me, with the unhappy wording typical of the very shy, whether I wanted to leave as badly as he did.

I said, laughing, that I did, but that I had come with someone else and couldn't go until my friend also was ready to depart: we only had the one car between us.

'Ah,' the man said, also laughing. 'That's a shame, then we're both stuck.' (The word he used was *incastrati*, wedged, fitted.) 'Normally I could have offered you a lift, but this evening I'm without a car. Stupidly I went and crashed mine into the back of a Peugeot and knocked the headlights out. I'm a good driver as a rule, I can't think what got into me.'

I felt a funny tickling feeling . . . No, that is writer's shorthand, I didn't feel anything, just a stillness, a suspension mark, as if Fate had drawn an apostrophe in the air, bidding for my attention. Rome had two and a half million inhabitants, many with cars, many with French cars, several if not many with Peugeots: the chance was slender, and it was only chance, but somehow, if true, there was a significance about it, there had to be. 'And the Peugeot?' I asked, when the moment had passed. 'What happened to the Peugeot? Who did it belong to?'

'It belonged to some Belgian diplomat or other. He was very good about it, very civil. His car was much more seriously damaged than mine and he had to call a pick-up truck and have it towed to a garage. I'm afraid I spoilt his evening for him.'

No irony intended, but as things turned out the shy man on the terrace was to spoil quite a number of Charles's evenings in one way or another. In fact it was lucky for Charles that he had an amphibian's agility and a wandering disposition and soon hopped off to other ponds and stopped minding, because otherwise the count of spoilt evenings to date would be roughly in the region of twelve thousand, four hundred and twenty-four and still rising. It is tempting to say that, with a fairly long lapse since our Introduction, I had at last met up with love in the form I had been seeking, but this would be a romantic's view. My father's, for example, who used to be moved to tears by 'Some Enchanted Evening' in every rendering, even his own. No, the way I see it, with the symbol of the accident Fate was simply trying to tell me that as regards sentimental travel I was off the dodgem tracks now and on to the main highway. The actual meeting – well, that would depend (as it did for everyone, everywhere, always, *in saecula saeculorum*) on stamina and my ability to stick on course.

A NOTE ON THE AUTHOR

Amanda Prantera was born and brought up in East Anglia. She went to Italy for a brief holiday when she was twenty and has lived there ever since. She has written seven previous novels, the most recent of which is *The Kingdom of Fanes*.